'Twas the ... Ch...

Unlike the rhyme, h... ...tmas Eve
rarely have the luxury of quiet moments, but
whichever ward or clinic is involved they all
share in the anticipation and excitement
building up to the joys of Christmas Day.

Our four books this month are set in hospitals
during Christmas Eve, when emotions are
heightened, and our heroes and heroines are,
unexpectedly or not, forced to confront their
real feelings. We visit Casualty, Maternity,
Intensive Care and Paediatrics, and in the dark
hours of the night touch on sadness, humour
and joy, before facing the dawn of a wonderful
new day.

Merry Christmas!

A New Zealand doctor with restless feet, **Helen Shelton** has lived and worked in Britain, and travelled widely. Married to an Australian she met while on safari in Africa, she recently moved to Sydney, where they plan to settle for a little while at least. She has always been an enthusiastic reader and writer, and inspiration for the background for her medical romances comes directly from her own experiences working in hospitals in several countries around the world.

Recent titles by the same author:

CONTRACT DAD
A MATTER OF PRACTICE
POPPY'S PASSION

ONE MAGICAL KISS

BY
HELEN SHELTON

MILLS & BOON®

DID YOU PURCHASE THIS BOOK WITHOUT A COVER?

If you did, you should be aware it is **stolen property** as it was reported
unsold and destroyed by a retailer. Neither the author nor the publisher
has received any payment for this book.

*All the characters in this book have no existence outside the imagination
of the author, and have no relation whatsoever to anyone bearing the
same name or names. They are not even distantly inspired by any
individual known or unknown to the author, and all the incidents are
pure invention.*

*All Rights Reserved including the right of reproduction in whole or in
part in any form. This edition is published by arrangement with
Harlequin Enterprises II B.V. The text of this publication or any part
thereof may not be reproduced or transmitted in any form or by any
means, electronic or mechanical, including photocopying, recording,
storage in an information retrieval system, or otherwise, without the
written permission of the publisher.*

*This book is sold subject to the condition that it shall not, by way of
trade or otherwise, be lent, resold, hired out or otherwise circulated
without the prior consent of the publisher in any form of binding or
cover other than that in which it is published and without a similar
condition including this condition being imposed on the subsequent
purchaser.*

*MILLS & BOON and MILLS & BOON with the Rose Device
are registered trademarks of the publisher.*

*First published in Great Britain 1998
Harlequin Mills & Boon Limited,
Eton House, 18-24 Paradise Road, Richmond, Surrey TW9 1SR*

© PoppyTech Ltd 1998

ISBN 0 263 81256 1

*Set in Times Roman 10 on 11½ pt.
03-9812-53095-D*

*Printed and bound in Norway
by AIT Trondheim AS, Trondheim*

CHAPTER ONE

THE medical superintendent's office was on the top floor of the new hospital's administrative building and, needing the exercise after the three-hour flight from Sydney and the drive from Wellington's airport out to the coast fifty kilometres north of the city, Will took the stairs.

When he pushed open the door into Jeremy's suite the director's secretary looked up with an automatically friendly smile but her expression warmed delightedly when she saw who it was.

'Will!' she exclaimed, rising to greet him. 'What a wonderful surprise.' Her eyes widened as she took in the three enormous stuffed toys he'd bought for Jeremy's children. 'They're beautiful,' she breathed, patting the koala while she eyed the kangaroo and its obese wombat friend. 'Wild, free creatures of the forest. The girls will adore them.'

She wore a crystal on a black leather thong around her neck and now she lifted it and peered at him through it. 'But, then, coming from you, *any* woman would adore them.' To his amusement she fluttered blue eyelashes at him. 'A joyful Christmas to you, Will. Your arrival is the crimson in my purple day. Jeremy wasn't expecting you to be flying back to us until after the holidays. How was Australia?'

'Hot.' Will deposited the toys beside her desk and suppressed his smile, returning her greeting instead with a guarded nod. He spent enough time in Jeremy's office to be on mildly friendly terms with the superintendent's secretary but that was all, and her dramatic enthusiasm for his company invariably left him faintly bemused. 'And Merry Christmas to you, too, Vivienne.'

Moving away from her desk, he had to duck to avoid an overhanging branch from an elaborately decorated Christmas tree and he realised that, including the huge specimen which had dominated the foyer downstairs, it was the third tree he'd seen in the building so far. 'Beautiful,' he remarked, meaning the pine itself and the fresh, woody fragrance of its needles, but she seemed to take his comment as a personal compliment.

'I have a gift for creating objects in harmony with nature,' she told him happily. 'Do you like my Santa?'

'Very nice.' He answered automatically then did a double take. The stuffed toy she'd referred to dominated the tree and squashed all the branches around it. Red and round, it was at least sixty centimetres high and it had unmistakable breasts.

'She's *Mother* Christmas,' Vivienne breathed. 'Because I believe that women have the power to do anything.'

'Of course they have.' Eyeing the rest of the unusual and expensive-looking baubles on the tree doubtfully, Will wondered how much it had all cost. Despite the fact that this hospital, the newest and supposedly most efficiently designed in New Zealand, had formally opened only eighteen months earlier, financial resources were already stretched and every ward, including the intensive care unit he himself was in charge of, had received a tersely worded memo early in December, reminding staff that Christmas decorations constituted 'an unnecessary expense of no measurable benefit' which this year 'would not be tolerated'.

'I believe that a woman should acknowledge her personal desires,' Vivienne was saying. She'd rolled back her chair and now crossed her legs beneath the long transparent skirt she wore and eyed him meaningfully. 'I believe we have a right to demand fulfilment of all of our personal ambitions.'

'Sounds like a very sensible approach,' Will said absently, looking around. It wasn't just the tree—the whole office was decorated, and he remembered that there'd been Christmas lights blinking as well as carols playing in the foyer. Clearly, he registered, the cash constraints which limited spending on the wards hadn't had the same impact when it came to facilities for the administrative staff.

'This world has been ruled far too long by ignorant and feeble men,' Vivienne added.

'I'm sure you're right.'

He checked his watch. There'd been no noise from the inner office and it occurred to him belatedly that he might have been assuming too much to expect the superintendent to still be on site at four o'clock on such a beautifully warm Christmas Eve afternoon. 'Is Jeremy in?'

'Alas, only for one more hour,' Vivienne said smoothly. 'Then he must fly away to finish his Christmas shopping. Will, I'd like you to know that I've always found you an extremely attractive man.'

'That's very sweet, Vivienne.' He wondered why he hadn't predicted this. 'And you're a lovely girl, but I'm seeing someone at present.'

'Oh.' She looked askance at him. 'I didn't know. Jeremy said that you were drifting alone through the universe.'

Will doubted that Jeremy would have used those exact words. 'Jeremy never knows as much as he thinks he knows,' he said dryly, although in this case, of course, there wasn't much for the other man to know. Yet. Will *wanted* to be seeing Maggie the way he'd meant Vivienne to assume, and he intended to begin seeing her that way, but so fra she'd proved difficult to persuade. 'I'll have a talk with him.'

Pleased that Vivienne appeared to shrug off his unavailability with equanimity, he reached for the inner door into Jeremy's office, but Vivienne immediately sprang into secretarial mode. 'You can't go in.' She moved and her hand came out swiftly to where he'd gripped the handle. She stroked one black-painted fingernail lightly across his wrist. 'Sorry. Jeremy said he didn't want their interaction disturbed. He's with Dr Miller. They're talking about next year's research assistant appointments.'

Will drew back his hand sharply. 'How long has she been in there?'

'Time is an abstract concept.' The secretary peered at him through her crystal again, her expression serene. 'I took herbal tea in fifteen minutes ago. Dr Miller's aura was shivering. I sensed she was upset.'

Will wasn't sure about Maggie's aura but he was very sure she'd be upset. Very upset. She'd put months of planning into her research plans for next year. Christmas Eve was a disastrous time for Jeremy to decide to tell her that her application for a research assistant had been rejected.

Jeremy had told him privately about the decision two weeks before, and because Will had been worried about how Maggie would take the rejection he'd made tentative approaches to drug companies about sponsorship, but he hadn't had any luck coming up with funds. Not that that meant Maggie wouldn't, he acknowledged. And he intended to encourage her to try.

But he couldn't say anything in front of Jeremy. Always desperate for funds for projects of his own, and totally ruthless when it came to money, Will wouldn't put it past his friend to approach the same companies himself if he thought there was any chance of success. Only in Jeremy's case, Will acknowledged grimly, instead of looking for research funds he'd be looking for sponsorship for some ludicrous corporate sporting event.

'And there are whispers that you have had approval for a research assistant for your own work, Will.' Vivienne was smiling at him again, her confidence obviously and happily undented. 'When I took in the tea Jeremy was telling Dr Miller that approval for your funding has come through.' Perhaps not getting enough information from her crystal, she put her hands up to her face and peered at him between her fingers. 'You must be very excited.'

'Relieved,' Will said wearily, wondering why he hadn't predicted that Jeremy would tell Maggie about his own successful approach. It would be one way that his friend, who hated conflict and arguments, would be able to make his own contribution to the decision not to chase funding seem minimal. No doubt he'd taken the opportunity to try and link the two events—Maggie losing her assistant and him, Will, gaining one—even though the superintendent knew as well as he did that the funding was entirely separate.

Although both he and Maggie were intensive care consultants, his background was in anaesthetics so he'd been able to obtain research funding from the university's anaesthetic department, whereas Maggie was a physician. Her research funding or, in this case, her lack of funding was due mostly to cutbacks within the department of medicine's budget.

However, even at the best of times, he conceded, with or without Jeremy's interference, he and Maggie were hardly confidants. Cool, very English and unfailingly reserved, her carefully maintained indifference towards him frequently grated at his nerves. Now, tired from the meetings and presentations which had kept him in Sydney for the last six days, he briefly considered delaying their meeting.

'He definitely said he didn't want to be disturbed.'
Vivienne fluttered her blue eyelashes at him again. 'Come
and let me show you through my Christmas tree,' she invited. 'Every decoration is a symbol of a special moment
in our planet's life.'

Will shook his head vaguely, distracted by thoughts of
Maggie, but the image of her made up his mind. It wasn't
important how tired he was—Maggie was one thing in the
place guaranteed to revive him. Besides, he'd been away
all week. He went for the door again. He wanted to see
her.

'I'll make you one of my special herbal teas,' Vivienne
offered urgently.

'No need.' Will twisted the handle. 'Jeremy's going to
have to put up with me interrupting.'

The superintendent was seated awkwardly behind his pa-
per-strewn desk, his head lowered, apparently pretending to
study the sheaf of documents he held. Characteristically, he
looked harassed and forlorn. His sandy hair was ruffled and
his round face was flushed and uncomfortable, but after a
brief, shrewdly assessing look Will's eyes went to Maggie.

She stood at the broad window at the side of the room,
facing away from him. Although he couldn't see her expression, her crossed arms and the tight set of her narrow
shoulders beneath the white doctor's coat she wore suggested that the encounter hadn't been going well. She
swung around seconds after he'd entered and her lovely
green eyes widened.

'Will! What on earth are you doing here?' Jeremy spoke
first and Will's brief glance back at him revealed that the
other man's face had quickly shed its careful hangdog look
and turned almost comical in his astonishment. 'I can't believe... You're back!'

'As scheduled,' he observed mildly, wondering why both

Jeremy and Vivienne had seemed to find his return so startling. Maggie, too, looked shocked. Always pale, her skin had turned ashen.

He nodded towards her. 'Maggie.'

'Will.'

Belying her obvious dismay, her greeting was even but still cool, and he berated himself for having entertained hopes of anything more. What had he expected? he asked himself cynically. That she'd missed him?

Their relationship had never been an easy one. Technically, as director of the intensive care unit of which she was deputy director, he was her immediate boss, but his appointment had only been made a year earlier and for the six months before that she'd been the acting director. According to Jeremy, she'd accepted the job and the necessary transfer from England only after the superintendent, desperate to recruit her for his almost-finished hospital, had dropped what Will suspected had been exceedingly heavy hints about the top job eventually, formally, becoming hers.

But it hadn't worked out that way. She was a superb physician who'd led the unit's medical team with skill and integrity, yet behind the scenes Jeremy and other recruitment staff had approached him directly at the London hospital where he'd been working for five years and had offered him the position.

The idea had been tempting. His British hospital experience had been both enjoyable and useful but he'd been missing New Zealand and had been ready to come home. He hadn't known anything about Maggie at the time he'd agreed to take the job, but once he'd understood the situation and how she'd been misled he recognised that she must have been disappointed by his arrival.

To her credit she'd never allowed any hint of bitterness to impinge on their professional relationship even if his personal approaches towards her had always been firmly and coolly rebuffed—a reaction which had grown more frustrating the more he'd come to know her, he admitted. Her calm refusal to have anything to do with him aside from professionally drove him mad. He didn't consider himself particularly acquisitive or egotistical but he wasn't used to not getting what he wanted.

'Have you had a productive break?' she asked. Pale and delicate, as usual she wore her long red hair coiled into a silky knot on the top of her head.

Not for the first time he found himself wishing that the colour of her hair signalled a more flammable temperament. If she'd been bad-tempered, with any tendency to outbursts of emotion or passion, he might have worked harder to provoke her into an open confrontation where she could have voiced the resentments she must harbour about his appointment and so perhaps clear the air between them. But, as far as he could see, her emotional control was supreme.

There were no chinks in Maggie Miller's armour. At least none that he'd found so far. Not that that meant he'd resigned himself to never finding any, he acknowledged. Not yet. He wanted her too much for that.

'A busy one,' he conceded, replying to her cool enquiry about his time away.

Something about his answer seemed to displease her because her beautiful mouth tightened and she tilted her little chin up towards him almost defensively. 'There was no reason for you to rush back from your holiday. I'd already agreed to cover your Boxing Day duties, which means you had until the twenty-ninth. I believe in the past I've proved myself fairly capable—'

'I've never questioned your capabilities,' he interjected, torturing himself by imagining how she'd react now if he took that tense little chin and lifted it higher so he could kiss her. The idea of her biting him wasn't off-putting, but the infinitely more likely outcome of her reeling away in disgust was.

'And I wasn't on holiday,' he added wearily. On the contrary, the week had been hard work. 'My meetings didn't finish until late last night. This was the earliest I could get back.'

Her unblinking regard suggested that she doubted it and he added more tightly, 'As far as I was concerned, there was never any doubt about my return. I never expected you to cover any of my on-call duties apart from those we'd already arranged. You knew that I was flying back today.'

'I was told that your plans would be changing.' She sent the medical director a telling look. 'Jeremy—'

'I asked Maggie to cover,' Jeremy said gloomily. 'Be reasonable, Will,' he countered, his tone lifting and becoming defensive when Will turned his narrowed regard to his fellow anaesthetist. 'A good-looking, single man like you on the loose in Sydney in a heat wave? All those beautiful beaches and beautiful girls in bikinis? I was sure you'd take advantage of the holiday season to stay on a few days this time. We thought you'd be away until after next week at least.'

'Or even longer,' Maggie offered smoothly, her expression suggesting that she'd hoped for that much at least.

'Happily, you were both wrong,' Will said edgily. Sydney had been hot and he acknowledged that if he'd had either the time or the inclination to visit any of the city's beaches he'd have found them full of the beautiful bikini-clad women Jeremy had referred to. Perhaps, in the distant past, in the days when the pair of them had shared a flat as medical students, he might have been tempted. But not now. Jeremy and, no doubt, Maggie herself might have difficulty believing it but as far as he was concerned the most important thing in his life now was his work. His work, and the responsibility that went with his position.

Besides, he didn't want young girls in bikinis.

'And I'm here now.' He gave his friend another hard look, relenting only when Jeremy had the grace to look appropriately sheepish. 'Maggie, about these research assistants—'

'Jeremy's already explained,' she said thinly, as she moved from the window, the movement drawing his attention to the soft curve of her thighs outlined by the pale fabric of the dress she wore under her white coat. 'I understand everything.'

Her pointed look took in Jeremy as much as him and, though Will met her eyes with resignation, he caught the other man's pained wince.

'Congratulations on getting your new assistant,' she continued, her lovely mouth controlled again although something less cool in the depths of the green gaze that brushed him made him tense.

He tilted his head, immediately alert, his eyes narrowing on hers, but promptly, as if she'd sensed his interest and it bothered her, the glimmer extinguished.

He went towards her. 'Maggie, wait. We should talk about this—'

'Forget it, Will. As usual there's no point. Goodbye, gentlemen. Happy Christmas, both of you.' She dodged his outstretched arm and reached the door he'd closed. 'I suppose you can consider your new research assistant a reluctant Christmas present from me.'

'Maggie—'

But she shut him out, the quiet forcefulness of the way the door closed fully reflecting the calm bitterness behind her last words.

Will studied his mute friend tersely. 'Thanks a bundle, Jerry.'

His friendship with Jeremy was largely a product of the length of time they'd known each other. They'd been at school together, primary and secondary, and later had trained as anaesthetists at the same time, first at Otago, New Zealand's southern university, then in Wellington. He liked the other man usually, even if he didn't approve of the enthusiasm with which he had taken to his new administrative appointment, but he wasn't blind to his faults. 'What the hell was all that nonsense about girls in bikinis?'

'How was I to know you wouldn't want to stay on?' Jeremy protested. 'You haven't had a holiday all year and you deserve some fun. I told you not to hurry back. I thought I was doing you a favour, by organising for Maggie to cover for you.'

'You weren't.' He remembered Maggie's expression. Her opinion of him had never been high but, thanks to Jeremy, it'd probably plunged to an all time disaster level. 'What is it with you?' he demanded. 'Why on earth would you assume I'm even going to be remotely interested in chasing around after strange women in bikinis?'

'Perhaps because the grass always seems greener?' Jeremy suggested lamely.

'Hasn't it ever occurred to you that I might envy you?'

'What?' His friend blinked at him like a bemused guinea pig. 'You? You're kidding. Envy me what?'

Will sighed. 'Think about it, Jerry. You've got a lovely wife, a beautiful home, three delightful children—'

'A mortgage the size of Mount Cook, a wife who spits tacks if I'm ten minutes late home from footie practice and three terrors who tried to set fire to the only babysitter stupid enough to agree to look after them for a night,' Jeremy countered glumly. 'Come on, Will. Cut it out. You think I wouldn't trade places?'

'Not even for a day,' Will said dryly. Catherine ran Jeremy's life like clockwork and his friend adored her. He was devoted to her and the girls and right now that devotion seemed like just about the superintendent's only redeeming feature. 'You wouldn't trade your life for the world.'

'Don't bet on it,' his friend said miserably.

'Jeremy—'

'OK, I couldn't live without Catherine,' he added unhappily. 'But, still, I know that if I were still single I wouldn't be rushing back from Sydney, not if I had your pulling power. Remember the fun we had that year—'

'We were students. Practically adolescents. Things are different now.'

'I don't see why,' his friend declared. 'Not for you. There's no reason why you still shouldn't enjoy—'

'There're dozens of reasons,' Will countered roughly. 'Number one being that that's not how I choose to lead my life.'

'Why?' Jeremy blinked up at him in apparent bemusement. 'Because you're still lusting after the delectable Dr Miller?'

Will ignored him. 'Did you have to give her the bad news about losing her assistant on Christmas Eve?'

'Not my fault.' The other man lifted his arms in a semi-helpless gesture as if to say, 'Women!' 'She demanded to know, practically forced it out of me. What could I do? The decision was made weeks ago. Was I supposed to keep pretending I still didn't know?'

'For a start.' Will said heavily. 'You knew how important this was to her. Couldn't you have held off on ruining her Christmas?'

He found himself going to the window. Subconsciously,

he realised, he must have been keeping track of the time it would take Maggie to get to the ground floor of the building because he caught sight of her just as she emerged below him.

A concrete path snaked from the main doors across a broad, newly mown lawn to the ward block but, instead of heading directly away along it, as he'd expected, she took a sharp detour right and marched straight onto the lawn and towards a knee-high stack of fresh clippings someone had piled near the middle of it.

To his astonishment, when she reached it she lifted one small, immaculately shod foot then, not even taking the time to look around and check that she was unobserved, kicked out viciously and sent the fragments flying. Despite his shock, Will only just stopped himself from laughing out loud. He watched her appreciatively, enjoying himself enormously.

Once she had the grass flattened she stepped back and eyed the scattered grass with what looked to him like definite satisfaction. To his mingled amusement and resignation, though, she then went for a rake the gardener must have left against the wall of the building and immediately began to scrape the clippings back into a neat pile again.

'At least you could have had the decency to tell her that me getting a research assistant had nothing to do with her losing hers,' he said absently to Jeremy. 'You know the funding is completely separate. She obviously thinks I had something to do with this.'

'You can handle it,' Jeremy said blithely, coming over to where Will stood. 'You know what a wimp I am when it comes to women. Frankly, Maggie terrifies me and I've never even heard her raise her voice. Your shoulders are broader. What on earth's she doing?'

'Tidying the lawn,' Will said softly, not elaborating.

'You know you were the one who wouldn't fight for the extra funding.'

'The department of medicine's already fully committed for next year,' Jeremy countered. 'There's nothing I can do.'

'That BMW they've given you would cover the salaries of two assistants as well as a cheap replacement car,' Will observed pointedly, still watching Maggie far below as she finished reassembling the grass.

'That car's part of my package,' Jeremy said quickly. 'Besides, I need it. The sedan's too small now that Catherine's pregnant again. Also, it's a solid, safe car. A man needs that when he's got four children to protect.' He was quiet for a few seconds. 'Lovely legs,' he said finally, when Maggie had replaced the rake and moved off again. 'She's exquisite, isn't she?'

At the hard look Will sent him the other man promptly blanched. He pulled back, lifting his hands defensively. 'OK, OK,' he said. 'I get the message. Forget I said anything.'

'You're a married man,' Will grated, pulling back himself as he realised that what they'd both been doing effectively amounted to spying on the other doctor.

'Marriage doesn't mean I'm not going notice a woman like Maggie Miller.' Apparently finding that thought depressing, Jeremy's face turned glum again. 'So?' Obviously the distance he'd put between them reassured the other man because he pushed again. 'Had any luck?'

'What do you think?' Will regarded his friend heavily, irritated by his easy assumption that their long association gave him a right to expect any insight into his personal affairs. 'You haven't exactly done your best to help that along,' he growled.

Jeremy shrugged. 'Not like you to need any help.'

'Assuming I'm interested.'

'Ha. Ha.' Jeremy didn't even make a token attempt to hide his disbelief. 'If that look you just gave me meant you're not interested, then I sure as hell don't want to be around when you are.'

'I'm busy.'

'Since when did work ever get in the way of your love life?'

'Drop it, Jerry.' Sending his friend a meaningful look, he deliberately changed the subject to the original purpose of his visit. 'I bought the girls Christmas presents from Australia.' He was godfather to Jeremy's eldest daughter but he always bought gifts for her two sisters as well. 'Some toys. Vivienne's looking after them. Tomorrow I want to make up for some of the time I've missed this week, by catching up on paperwork. I probably won't get time to call by to see Catherine and the girls until after Christmas.'

'OK.' Jeremy nodded. 'They were hoping to see you, but not expecting it. I warned them you'd be staying on in Sydney.'

He rolled his eyes at Will's impatient look. 'All right, all right,' he said appeasingly. 'I'll explain you're working. But if you get a spare few hours you know where we'll be. On TV last night they were predicting twenty-eight degrees for tomorrow with hardly any wind so we'll be at the beach all day.'

Will nodded. Jeremy owned a holiday house at Waikanae, a settlement a few miles further north up the picturesque Kapiti coast. It wasn't far from the hospital and Will often called in on him and his family when they stayed up there.

Will's own large family was mostly Auckland-based— around an hour's flying time or a seven-hour drive away—

and while he'd normally have gone up for a few days over Christmas this year, because of his Sydney trip and the fact that he was on call for ICU on Boxing Day, he'd decided to leave visiting until the New Year.

'We're having the traditional Christmas barbecue, and Catherine's dad's bringing up a load of frozen whitebait,' Jeremy continued, referring to the tiny New Zealand fish traditionally bound in batter and cooked in small fritters. 'All the relatives will be there so there'll be plenty of food around if you change your mind at the last minute.'

'I'll remember.' Will was at the door, and he lifted his arm in acknowledgement of the invitation. 'Give Catherine my love.'

Hoping to catch up with Maggie, he went directly from Jeremy's office to the intensive care unit. His excuse was that he wanted to give her the details he'd collected about alternative funding for her research assistant but privately he recognised that his motivation was far more complex. Now that he knew for sure that the infuriating serenity she wore like a shield was far thinner than she wanted him to believe, he wanted to look at her. He wanted to know what else she hid from him.

She wasn't in the unit but Ian, one of his registrars, looked up when he came in. His mouth widened into a relieved smile, suggesting that he was glad to see him. Wearing a sterile gown and gloves, he was seated behind a guard-covered, unconscious and ventilated patient, holding a gauze swab to the man's neck and another just below his collarbone.

'Hi, Dr Saunders,' he called, waving for him to come over. 'Good to see you back. This is Mr Fale. We're trying to Swan him but I've just hit the artery twice in a row, trying for the subclavian. Steven's already tried the right internal jugular with no luck,' he added, naming the veins they'd been trying to cannulate while he nodded to the SHO who stood beside him. 'Any chance you've got a spare minute to take over?'

'Sure.' Will took a mask from the box close to the bed and fastened it around his face. To Swan a patient meant to insert a Swan-Ganz catheter, a special type of central intravenous line adapted for taking specialised temperature and pressure readings. 'Come with me while I scrub. What's the indication for a Swan?'

Steven took over, applying pressure to the puncture sites, while Ian came with him to the clinical room. 'Fifty-four-year-old man four days post-op after a Hartmann's for a perforated tumour,' he explained, referring to the procedure where the segment of tumour-affected bowel was excised and a colostomy, or drainage loop of bowel, was formed.

'He went into VT on one of the surgical wards this afternoon, then VF arrest,' he added, indicating that the patient's heart had gone into an abnormal rhythm then stopped working.

Ian unpacked a sterile box containing a towel for Will to use to dry his hands. 'Looks like it's all secondary to infection. Dr Miller checked out his heart with the echo machine and it looks OK, but Microbiology's found gram-negative rods in his urine and blood.' Gram-negative rods signified a type of bacteria commonly found in urinary infections, but the results suggested that the infection was in his blood as well.

'We're having trouble keeping his blood pressure up and his kidneys working, even though we've given him loads of fluids and full support. Dr Miller decided we need to Swan to work out exactly what's going on.'

Will nodded. There'd been controversy in recent years in the anaesthetic and general medical literature about the usefulness of the catheter, and the consensus seemed to be that they were overused in ICUs, but in this situation he understood why Maggie had ordered one. Overwhelming infection could damage virtually any organ and the Ganz would give them vital information about the functioning of Mr Fale's heart and lungs, information they now needed to manage him and his medications properly. 'What about his tumour?'

'The surgeons are still keen for full treatment. He's middle-aged but active and the liver was clear at operation. Although the full pathology report isn't through yet, the lymph nodes felt clear. They think that even at worst, and they do contain tumour, he still probably has a good few years ahead of him.'

'Which makes it worthwhile,' Will agreed. Gowned now, he pulled on the gloves the registrar had opened for him. 'You said that Maggie had been up with the echo. Was that just now?'

'A few hours ago. I think she's gone across to one of the obstetric wards. The obstetricians have admitted a woman with pre-eclampsia. Dr Miller wanted to take a look at her in case things go wrong quickly.'

'How does she sound?'

'According to the registrar, very dodgy. They've been watching her for the past week as an outpatient and she's been on bed rest but there's been no improvement. She's only thirty-one weeks so they were hoping to hold off on doing an emergency Caesarean, but they might not have any choice.'

Will nodded. Pre-eclampsia, or toxaemia of pregnancy, was potentially disastrous for both mother and baby, and if it progressed it still occasionally proved fatal.

Ian came with him to the bed and Steven scrambled aside to give him access to their patient's left side. 'Since he's positioned I'll try once more for a subclavian,' Will said quietly, nodding his thanks when the SHO removed the sterile guard from the trolley holding the Ganz. 'If that doesn't work we'll go for a femoral vein.'

Using a one-mil syringe Will gently inflated the tiny balloon at the end of the catheter to make sure it was working, then he let the balloon go flat again. There were four different tiny tubes inside the main one and he checked that each had been flushed with heparinised saline to prevent blood clotting inside them, and then he injected ice-cold sterile dextrose into the temperature-sensitive line to confirm that that was working too.

The site below the patient's collar-bone and up into his neck had already been cleaned but Will used a swab to re-coat the skin with iodine solution, before puncturing the skin just below Mr Fale's collar-bone. He advanced the needle until he was below the bone, then moved it inwards towards his patient's neck.

He felt a very slight pop as the needle advanced into the vein, much less resistance than he would have encountered if, like Ian, he'd accidentally pierced the artery, and the blood that flashed promptly back into his syringe was reassuringly dark.

'Venous,' Ian breathed, obviously relieved. 'Finally.'

Will carefully threaded a guide wire up through the middle of the hollow cannula which he then withdrew, replacing it with a specialised introducing cannula designed to go with the Ganz. He pulled out the wire then slowly inserted the catheter, studying the pressure readings its sensitive recording equipment now sent back to the computerised monitor beside them as he guided the line into place.

He wanted the tip of the line to sit in the pulmonary artery, the vessel just through the right ventricle of the heart. Each different vessel and part of the heart sent back a characteristic pressure signal, meaning he could be sure where the line was.

After it had passed from the right atrium of the heart into the right ventricle, Ian and Steven adjusted the bed so that Mr Fale's head was upright again, and then Will slid the line through the ventricle into the pulmonary artery. He blew up the balloon and let it float until it wedged in a smaller vessel, watching the monitor as it printed out a narrow strip of the results the Ganz sent back.

'He needs a routine chest X-ray to check its position,' Will ordered, 'but it looks good. Got anything to suture this with?'

'I'll do it, Dr Saunders.' Steven, the SHO, was still scrubbed and sterile and he nodded his willingness. 'And I've got a dressing here. Thanks.'

'Yes, thanks a lot,' said Ian. 'Sorry to have to scream for help.'

'It's what I'm here for,' Will said evenly, not bothered. Both Ian and Steven were good, hard-working and capable doctors. Ian was senior and it was rare for him to require assistance with such routine ICU tasks, and Will was happy to help out if he was needed. 'Ian, you look tired,' he observed. 'Busy night on call last night?'

The registrar shook his head. 'I'm on tonight. It's not work that's making me tired at the moment—it's home. Emily's teething but she's been ill with a viral upper respiratory thing. The GP's been calling in a couple of times a day, even though he claims not to be particularly worried about her, but it's been hard on Annabel. We've managed to organise a monitor for the cot and everything but she still can't relax. She's a bit better when I'm there but it's still not easy. She keeps insisting that one of us gets up every hour to check on her. Emily was a bit less snuffly this morning so, hopefully, she's on the mend.'

Will listened sympathetically. Emily was Ian's and Annabel's second-born child but he knew that their first had died two years earlier with a diagnosis of sudden infant death syndrome so he understood why they were both so concerned about what was probably a minor illness. 'When are you due to finish here?' he asked. 'Nine tomorrow?'

'Hopefully in plenty of time to get home to cook Christmas dinner,' Ian confirmed. 'Both our families are coming in the evening and Annabel's so stressed out that I've promised to cook.'

'What are you tonight? First on?'

'Steven's on here in the unit but I'm first on after him for ICU plus I'm second on for Theatres and Maternity,' Ian told him, meaning that he would be the first doctor who'd be called for problems in the intensive care unit— Steven, although acting as official first on, was too junior still to be on duty without supervision—and the second called for anaesthetics, meaning he'd only be called to administer an anaesthetic if there was more than one emergency case or maternity patient needing surgery or an epidural at the same time. When he was away from the unit for any of those duties Steven would call the on-call consultant for emergency backup.

'Take me around the patients here,' Will instructed, making up his mind quickly. He had two invitations to Christmas parties for that evening but had no particular enthusiasm for either of them. 'After that you can go home,' he told him. 'I'll stay on and cover you overnight.'

'What?' The younger man looked astonished. 'Really?'

'It's no big deal.' Will shrugged. 'I'm happy to stay.'

'Well, thanks very much,' Ian said delightedly. 'Thanks, Dr Saunders, that's amazing. Annabel will be over the moon.'

'I'm glad.' Having now shed his gown and gloves, Will

directed Ian towards their patients. 'Let's go round. So, who else is on call tonight?'

'Dr Miller's consultant on,' Ian said promptly.

Maggie. Will smiled. 'I see Mr Radcliffe is still with us,' he remarked. 'What's been happening with his heart failure since I've been away?'

CHAPTER TWO

MAGGIE strode stiffly from the garden beneath Jeremy Donaldson's office directly to the hospital's obstetric unit. She paused outside, scraping her small feet efficiently on the wire mat in front of the door to shed a few spears of newly mown grass which still clung to her shoes, all the while berating herself furiously for having handled that meeting so poorly.

When she looked up again she promptly stiffened, half-startled by the serene image reflected back at her from the mirrored entrance doors.

It was one of her few strengths, she acknowledged grimly. Her face's at times miraculous indifference to any turmoil which blazed inside her still amazed her. Reassured, she clutched at that. It reminded her that regardless of how violently she'd reacted inwardly to Will turning up like that, and despite his watchfulness, in all likelihood he had no idea what seeing him unexpectedly like that had done to her.

That ignorance was something she was determined to preserve, she reminded herself. She pushed open the doors and went inside. Despite the fact that instead of fluently and maturely expressing her anger at the clear swap he and his great pal the medical superintendent had engineered to veto her research assistant, she'd acted like some sort of absurd frightened *duck*!

But, then, as Will pretty much always managed to effect some sort of bizarre upset in her equilibrium, she should stop punishing herself, learn to live with it and just get on with her work.

Of course, it hadn't helped that Jeremy Donaldson had been so convinced that Will wouldn't be back before Christmas that he'd managed to convince her. It hadn't helped either that before Will's unannounced arrival in his office the superintendent had spent most of their meeting describing some debauched rugby trip the two men had gone on years earlier when it sounded as if the pair of them had spent the entire week inside their respective hotel rooms, having sex with a succession of desperately eager women.

Maggie's mouth tightened. Knowing the two men, she was fully prepared to put Jeremy's own claims down to wishful thinking and a vivid imagination. As for Will, though, given not just his dark good looks but the full powerful effect of his personality, the story was entirely believable.

Not that that bothered her, she told herself firmly, briefly doing her best to feign blithe unconcern. But she *was* bothered. She knew that. However hard she strove not to be, however hard she strove for distaste, or even indifference, she knew that Jeremy's revelations about Will had provoked neither of those emotions in her.

But to concede her curiosity, let alone shavings of a disturbingly voyeuristic fascination at the thought of him making love, wouldn't get her anywhere, she told herself thickly. Even to acknowledge that she'd felt such a thing would be too appalling for words.

She let the unit's door swing shut heavily behind her. Will Saunders was an extraordinarily attractive man, she told herself defensively. It made sense that there'd be women who'd find themselves extraordinarily attracted to him, but she certainly wasn't ever going to let him have what he wanted from her. She wasn't immune to Will's attractions on a purely fantasy basis but, for what felt like the umpteenth time, she reminded herself that her marriage had left her with a profound indifference about the sex act itself and absolutely no curiosity to further her experience.

While she might occasionally indulge herself with a little…harmless intellectual speculation, she'd never seriously worried that she might physically succumb to him. He'd never concealed the fact that he wanted her but she simply didn't need the complications.

Nothing had changed, she told herself grimly. Just because she'd spent the week he'd been in Sydney missing him more than she'd ever missed anything in her life didn't mean anything had changed.

She took the stairs, rather than wait for the lift to take her up to the antenatal wards. Dodging a sparely decorated, plastic Christmas tree which leaned forlornly against the far dim corner of the top foyer, she went directly to Snell Ward's nursing station on the fourth floor.

The charge nurse, a tall woman in a dark blue uniform who wore a band of silver tinsel slung around her neck and a floppy red hat with MERRY CHRISTMAS embroidered in yellow cotton on her head, was studying a chart.

Maggie introduced herself. 'Maggie Miller,' she explained. 'I'm one of the ICU consultants. Mr Barnes called me about one of his admissions. A woman with pre-eclampsia…?'

'Mrs Everett. I'll take you to see her, Dr Miller.' The charge nurse had a friendly smile. 'She's in room four. The registrar's still with her and she'll have all the notes.'

The walls of the ward had been strung with colourful paper chains of pleated crêpe paper, and Maggie smiled at them. 'How on earth did you manage to get Christmas decorations over this side?' she asked. 'We were forbidden them on our wards.'

'We paid for everything out of our own little pockets.' They exchanged exasperated looks. 'It's only a few chains and one little tree but it makes things at least a wee bit brighter for the poor women who end up stuck in here over Christmas. You're not going to believe it but we've already had two visits from people in Accounts, wanting explanations.'

'I believe it.' Maggie rolled her eyes. For a relatively new hospital, the penny-pinching that went on was awe-inspiring. An accountant-like person had even questioned her recently about the type of soap she used. The hospital-issue soap reacted badly with her skin so when she had to wash her hands frequently, such as between patients in ICU or in Outpatients, she supplied her own solution. She'd always bought it herself, although the accountant-person hadn't been convinced until she'd produced receipts showing her personal credit card number. 'I *really* believe it,' she said grimly.

The registrar emerged from the room just as Maggie went to open the door to which the charge nurse had directed her. Maggie knew the younger doctor from having shared the occasional medical clinic in the past, and they greeted each other easily.

'Twenty-nine-year-old primigravida,' the registrar explained, referring to her patient's age and the fact that she was in her first pregnancy. 'A desperately wanted baby. Dates slightly unclear but she's about thirty-one weeks based on her earlier scans, although on Mr Barnes's scan today it looks as if baby is small for dates. Ideally we'd like to avoid surgery tonight and aim for a semi-elective Caesarean under epidural in Wellington once she's had

forty-eight hours of steroids to try and mature baby's
lungs.'

'What's her blood pressure doing now?'

'One-seventy over one-ten on admission. We started the
hydralazine infusion you suggested to Mr Barnes and she's
come down slowly to 156 over 98, according to the monitor, so that's a pretty good response.'

'How's her urine?'

'Her nurse has put in a catheter and she's passing around
fifty mils an hour. The urine she collected at home yesterday showed that she's losing about ten grams of protein a
day. We're waiting on biochemistry to find out how her
renal function is today but yesterday both her plasma urea
and creatinine were up. Her swelling's bad, there's fluid up
to her abdomen and back.'

Maggie nodded. The urine findings and blood results and
swelling were consistent with the leaky kidneys and blood
vessels which were a feature of pre-eclampsia. 'Platelets?'

'Within normal limits, as are her liver enzymes.' The
registrar touched her wooden clipboard quickly, and
Maggie understood the reason for her relief. There was a
dangerous syndrome associated with pre-eclampsia where
liver function and blood clotting were deranged but, thank-
fully, that didn't appear to be the case here.

'How about neuro-wise?'

'Headache,' the registrar said, 'which came on before the
hydralazine. Also, I think she's a bit twitchy. She's on regular neuro obs.'

'I'll take a look,' Maggie reassured her. 'Are you finished with the notes?'

'Let me fill in a couple of things.' The registrar's bleeper
shrilled and she lifted her hand to the speaker to muffle its
sound. 'I need to scout around for her old records and chase
up the rest of her results then I'll bring them in to you.'

Maggie pushed open the room door gently, waiting a few seconds for her eyes to accustom themselves to the dimness of the room after the harsh fluorescent lighting in the rest of the ward.

The curtains in the room were drawn. Linda Everett lay on her side and her bed was tipped so that the head was higher than the foot. Her eyes were closed. A blood-pressure cuff surrounded her right upper arm and its reading was displayed in red on a monitor next to the bed. There was a drip in her arm, connected to a pump, and a monitor used to monitor uterine contractions and the baby's heart-beat sat on a table beside it, the soft scratching of the needle recording the measurement the only sound in the room apart from the intermittent 'whoosh' of the blood pressure cuff filling.

'She's not asleep.' The staff nurse who stood at the bed-side touched her arm. 'Dr Kayo's just given her some pain relief. Are you the medical doctor?'

'Maggie Miller,' Maggie confirmed. She thanked the nurse for the chart she passed her and ran her eyes briefly down the blood pressure, pulse and urine output measure-ments, which all confirmed the information the registrar had already given her.

She touched their patient's shoulder. 'Mrs Everett?' she said gently. 'Hello. I'm Dr Miller.'

'Mmm.' Linda Everett's eyes came slowly open and she swivelled around onto her back. 'Hello. My head...?'

'The other doctor's just put some painkiller into your drip,' the nurse explained. 'It'll start working soon. Try and relax.'

'My baby...?'

'Is doing fine,' Maggie said softly, glancing towards the monitor. The baby's heart rate was healthily high and variable. She wasn't an expert in the field but she was confident that there were no overt signs of distress.

After explaining what she was going to do, she drew her ophthalmoscope out of the pocket of her white coat. She brought the small instrument close to her, watching how each of Linda's eyes reacted, then she turned the light on and checked the pupils' response as she shone it into each in turn. 'Keep looking at the corner of the ceiling above the door,' she instructed softly. Starting from the side of the bed then drawing closer to the patient's right eye so that their faces almost touched, she peered into one retina through the ophthalmoscope's small lens. 'That's right. Good. Keep watching the corner.'

She repeated her examination on the other side, then drew back, pleased. 'Fine,' she said reassuringly. It wasn't normal for the eyes to be damaged or the brain to be dangerously swollen in pre-eclampsia, but it was important to check.

She took out a small rubber-headed reflex hammer, nodding her thanks when the nurse moved to sweep back the covers at the end of the bed so that she could lift her patient's knees from the mattress. Maggie tested Linda's response at her knees and ankles, then her triceps and biceps on the left—her right arm was obstructed by the blood pressure cuff—then at both wrists. Finally she held her patient's chin gently and tapped her own thumb, testing Linda's jaw jerk.

She quickly completed a neurological examination, checked heart and lungs, and listened for bruits, or turbulence, in the arteries in the neck, against the eyes and at the back along the path of the renal arteries.

'Are you allergic to anything?' Maggie asked. 'Any history of asthma, or problems with anaesthetics?' Her patient

shook her head. 'Has anyone in the family ever had problems with anaesthetics?'

'Not that I know of,' Linda Everett said huskily. 'I've
never even been in hospital before. My husband...?'

'Has just run across to the canteen for a cup of tea,' the
nurse answered. 'He won't be long.'

Maggie straightened. 'I've finished now. I'll let you get
some rest.' When their patient's eyes lowered, Maggie
called the staff nurse to one side.

'Her reflexes are very brisk,' she said quietly. 'It's possible that that's related to the hydralazine but it might indicate increased risk of a seizure. I'll talk with Mr Barnes
and suggest he starts phenytoin to try and prevent that.'

'Her blood pressure's come down so won't that be
enough to stop her fitting?'

'We bring that down to try and stop brain haemorrhages,'
Maggie explained softly. 'The seizures themselves seem to
be independent of the blood pressure and can happen anyway.'

'Will she be going to ICU?'

'At present she can stay here. The move would be too
disturbing when the most important thing is that she stays
calm and quiet. If anything changes I'll reconsider.'

The registrar was waiting outside with the notes and
Maggie explained her findings as they went back to the
nursing station where she'd be able to telephone Mr Barnes.

As she'd half suspected from the conversation they'd had
earlier, the other consultant was reluctant to start anti-
convulsant medication without more to go on. 'I'd like to
hold off in case the reflexes are just due to the hydralazine,'
he told her. 'I didn't think she was particularly twitchy
when I examined her earlier but I'll review her again in a
few hours and reconsider.'

'I'm on call tonight for the ICU so call me directly if

there are any problems,' Maggie told the registrar firmly, once she'd finished speaking with the obstetrician. She gave the other doctor her personal bleeper number. 'I'm worried about her. I'll warn the ICU staff that she's around. I think that even if you manage to get away with an elective delivery in a few days post op the safest course would be for her to come to ICU either here or in Wellington directly from Theatre for twenty-four hours at least. Even if things look good that would seem wise.'

Delivery was part of the treatment for pre-eclampsia but it also signalled the most dangerous time for the patient, particularly the immediate post-delivery hours when the blood pressure could be very labile and when seizures were likely to occur. Over the years Maggie had seen several cases where the doctors had managed to save the baby only to lose the mother following the birth. She didn't know the New Zealand figures, but her memory of the UK ones was that about one in fifty women who developed the disease died.

'OK, Dr Miller.' The registrar waited while Maggie finished writing her recommendations in the notes, then came with her to the end of the ward. 'I hope you have a happy Christmas.'

'You, too.' Smiling, Maggie held up crossed fingers. 'Are you on tonight?'

'Tonight and tomorrow and Boxing Day,' the younger woman said ruefully. 'I'm trying to get my hours up well before my exams.'

'Poor you.' Maggie nodded a farewell. 'Still, it's holiday time now. With any luck, it'll be quiet.' Hopefully, the same would go for ICU, Maggie thought, going down the stairs. With Will away all week she'd had to work more than her usual share of nights on call and she decided she'd appreciate a low-stress evening.

Not that she begrudged covering for her colleague, she acknowledged, honesty forcing her to admit that, however convenient it might have been to use the fact against him. Over the eleven months he'd been Unit Director he'd worked more than his share of nights, including covering her for three weeks over Easter when she'd gone back to England to visit her mother.

She still owed him for that, she remembered, vowing to try and correct the imbalance despite his refusal so far to allow her to do so. Even if he didn't mind, she didn't like the thought of being in debt to him.

Rather than take the second-storey internal link across to the surgical and medical block, she went all the way to the ground floor and outside, wanting some fresh air. It was after five but still warm and balmy, with only a very light northerly breeze blowing—barely enough to disturb the strands of hair at her forehead.

Sheltered by a range of mountains from the cold southerly winds, which frequently buffeted Wellington itself, she'd noticed that temperatures in the region around the hospital were frequently at least a few degrees higher than those listed in the newspapers for the city. The past week had been glorious, sunny and calm, each day warmer than the one before.

It was her second southern hemisphere Christmas, but it had only taken one for her to decide that she definitely preferred celebrating the feast in summer. Crunchy frosts and roast chestnuts had their place in England, but here she was very content with beaches and picnics.

She started towards the ward block then stopped, not used to having nothing demanding her immediate attention. As patients were understandably reluctant to sit around in Outpatients on Christmas Eve, all clinics had finished before lunch. The only thing left on her timetable was the routine round they always did of the ICU patients at six but that still left her forty minutes.

The sound of her name being called brought her head up sharply. When she saw Will coming towards her she stiffened, the tiny hairs along the back of her arms standing up.

'Thanks for waiting,' he said softly when he reached her, the disturbingly shrewd narrowing of his blue eyes making her wonder, suddenly, if her expression was not quite the mask she'd assumed. 'You haven't been easy to track down.'

'I've been on Snell Ward.' Determined not to respond to what she saw as his baiting of her, she tilted her chin. 'Is this important, Will? I'm rather…' She wanted to say 'busy' but of course she couldn't so instead her words just trailed off.

She wished that he'd changed his clothes, before coming back to work. Instead of one of his usual suits, he still wore the pale open-necked shirt and easy-fitting faded blue jeans he'd had on in Jeremy's office, and neither did anything to conceal the powerful masculinity of the body beneath. Not liking the increasingly fast thud of the pulse in her chest, Maggie deliberately checked her watch again. She hoped the gesture looked pointed. 'Is there a problem on the unit?'

'Nothing acute that I'm aware of.' To her puzzlement he hauled two folded sheets of printed paper out of one of the back pockets of his jeans and passed them to her. 'I wanted to remind you that it might not be too late to find some private sponsorship for your research assistant.'

She blinked. 'What?'

'Before I had to leave for Australia I spoke with the reps whose names are underlined, but there're some I wasn't able to get hold of. They might be worth a try.'

'You've spoken to all these people?' She looked through the list, her mouth drying as she realised that the warmth of the sheets had come from being close to his body. 'Why would you do that?'

'Is it so unbelievable that I might want to help?'

'Yes.' She blinked again. 'I don't understand.' She thought they'd been in competition for funds. There were several ongoing research projects in the unit in which they were both involved, but she'd thought that it would suit him if the next year's major new research focus was his own interest. 'You wanted to help my research...?'

'I wanted to help you.'

Still she was puzzled. 'You mean...because having two major new studies in progress adds to the unit's prestige?'

'I mean because I know how much work you've put into this.' The impatient hardening of his gaze suggested she'd managed to exasperate him. 'Maggie, for once can't you just accept that I'm not the ruthless egotist you'd prefer me to be?'

'Ruthless' fitted him, she thought, but perhaps...perhaps not necessarily 'egotist'. 'I thought we were in competition for the funds,' she protested. 'Jeremy said—'

'Believe me, whatever Jeremy said makes no difference,' he interjected roughly. 'It has never made any difference. You're my deputy, Maggie. You and I are supposed to operate as a team. That's how it should be and it's certainly how I've always wanted it to be.'

'Well...thank you.' Lowering her head, Maggie studied the sheets he'd given her, still astonished. There were two pages of densely worded lists of companies and institutes, and over half the names were underlined. He'd obviously put considerable work into this and it was the last thing she'd ever have expected. 'I'll get onto it straight after Christmas.' She looked up at him solemnly. 'I don't know how to say...well, thank you.'

'You're welcome.' The eyes that looked down at her had softened. 'What are you doing tomorrow?'

'Tomorrow?' She frowned. The next day was Christmas Day. Was he worried that the unit wouldn't be adequately covered over the holiday? 'Well, I'm on call tonight,' she said slowly. 'Tomorrow I'll do an ICU round about nine with the day staff. Why? Do you want to come in for it?' She knew that he lived in Wellington proper rather than up here on the coast. 'I could make it an hour or so later if that would make it easier for you to get here.'

'I'm not talking about the unit, I'm talking about you. It's Christmas. What are you doing for lunch?'

'Lunch?' Aware that she kept echoing him and that she probably sounded ridiculous, she still couldn't help herself. 'I'm not sure I—'

'Lunch, Maggie.' He sounded impatient again. 'Look, I plan to be here, catching up on some work. I realise you don't have any family locally and I don't either. Christmas is family time. It occurred to me that you might not have made plans. I hadn't intended to take time off from work but, if you're not doing anything else, how about joining me for lunch?'

'Lunch,' she repeated.

'An hour or two by the beach,' he said. 'A break from here. I'll organise a picnic. It'll be fun. What do you think?'

Fun? Maggie retreated. 'No, I don't think so.'

Avoiding his frown, she looked down at the names he'd given her, and then back at him, wondering, now, about his motivation. She held the sheets out towards him in case he wanted them back. 'I'm very grateful for this, Will, but it doesn't mean that anything has changed. I mean, it was a very nice gesture but…' Her hands were shaking. 'Just because you've helped me here doesn't mean I'm going to…go out with you—'

The oath he uttered stopped her dead.

'Those names aren't a bribe,' he said rawly. The look that raked her was disgusted, and she caught her breath as he spun away from her. She wondered, sickly, if she'd misjudged him.

'Believe it or not, I was genuinely talking about lunch, Maggie—lunch. That's all. No obligations and no strings. Nothing to do with you finding a research assistant or those names, nothing to do with anything but a pleasant hour and some good food on Christmas Day.' He swore again. 'Forget it. Forget everything. I'm wasting my time.'

'Will…?'

The word came out urgently but involuntarily, and to her dismay it was enough to catch him as he strode away and enough to make him turn back. His face was hard, unreadable. 'Yes?'

'I'm sorry,' she said quietly, despite her nervousness, meaning it sincerely. There was no way his outrage could have been faked. 'I didn't mean to imply—'

'We both know exactly what you meant to imply, Maggie.'

Her breath jammed in her throat. 'Well, I'm sorry,' she repeated huskily.

'Then that makes two of us.'

He looked furious and she was guiltily aware that she deserved it, and that awareness was something she didn't like. She was used to feeling a mildly self-righteous resentment towards him, but now things seemed to have been reversed.

She didn't know what to say, how to make things better, and after a few tortured seconds he muttered, 'I've a theatre case to do—an abscess one of the surgeons wants to drain so it shouldn't take long, but I might be a few minutes late for the round. I've just seen most people with Ian so you can start without me.'

'I can take the round myself,' she said quickly, not even attempting to make sense out of why he'd agreed to take a case to Theatre when technically he should almost be off duty for the holiday. 'I'm on call tonight.' Embarrassed now, she didn't want to see him again so soon. 'I'll do the round myself,' she emphasised. 'I don't mind if you don't stay around.'

'You don't get away that easily, Maggie.' His blue glare seemed to see right through her. 'See you on the ward.' He turned away from her again and strode off towards the wards, leaving her shaking.

Mechanically she checked her watch. Five-thirty. Their encounter had taken barely ten minutes but it had left her reeling. She'd practically accused her boss of trying to bribe her into sleeping with him. What would happen now?

CHAPTER THREE

WILL'S anger about Maggie's accusation was genuine but it didn't last long. By the time he reached Theatres he was starting to see the amusing side of the encounter.

In fact, he decided, changing into baggy theatre pants and an ill-matching jerkin, he rather enjoyed having the advantage over her. No, not just *rather* enjoyed, he corrected himself *en route* to theatre two, *hugely* enjoyed. It was the first time it had ever happened, he thought with a grin. It wasn't going to be the last.

The case he'd agreed to cover because the first-on anaesthetic registrar was busy in Maternity was uncomplicated, an otherwise fit and healthy twenty-five-year-old man with a painful abscess which needed to be opened and drained.

Because the procedure was usually very short, rather than intubating his patient, which would involve sliding a tube into his airway, he simply used a mask which he attached via a reservoir bag to the anaesthetic machine and the nitrous oxide and oxygen mix he was using to keep him asleep.

Five minutes later when the surgeon had finished Will turned off the nitrous oxide, and when his patient came around he replaced the mask with a plastic one connected to a portable oxygen cylinder. While an orderly and one of the nurses helped transfer the man on his side onto a trolley, which the orderly had brought into the theatre, Will took control of the head of the operating table, controlling his patient's head and making sure that his oxygen mask stayed in place while he was moved.

He went with them to Recovery, finishing recording the details of the anaesthetic onto the blue-topped anaesthetic form which would go into the hospital notes as they arrived. 'Oxygen four litres a minute until he goes to the ward,' he instructed. 'He's had five of morphine at five-fifty so that should cover him for pain while he's here.'

'Great.' The recovery nurse beamed at him before she bent to confirm the details on the chart with the name and number on their sleepy patient's wrist-band. 'Hello, Matthew. Your operation's finished. Are you feeling all right?'

Matthew murmured his assent before his eyes drifted closed again.

The nurse looked back at Will. 'I'm surprised to see you doing this, Will. I thought Ian was second on tonight.'

'The roster changed,' he explained, checking his notes. 'I'm on till nine tomorrow.'

'How was Sydney? I heard it's been hot.'

'Thirty-four yesterday.'

'It'd be too much for me.' She switched their patient's tubing from the portable cylinder to the permanent supply behind the bed, adjusting the flow tap at the wall slightly. 'But it's good to see you back. We're having a little Christmas celebration after our nursing hand-over tonight,' she said lightly. 'Well, we will be if we're not too busy. I can't make any promises since it'll probably only amount to some cheap sparkling wine and a box of chocolates but we'd love you to come if you can make it.'

'I'll remember. Thanks.' Will signed his name with his characteristic scrawl then grinned at her. 'I see you've managed to smuggle in some Christmas decorations.' Each empty bed site was decorated with silver tinsel strips and the glass wall between Recovery and the main theatre corridor had been sprayed with mock snow and cheerful greetings. 'Isn't that looking for trouble?'

She laughed. 'We voted. We decided we were too important and that they wouldn't dare sack us all. We've got loads more decorations and even a tree of sorts ready to go up later. Aren't we brave?'

'Completely foolhardy,' he teased. They exchanged conspiratorial grins. 'Merry Christmas, Babs.'

'You, too, Will. Hope we see you later.'

But she called out his name a few seconds later as he was about to go into the changing room. 'Just thought it wouldn't be fair not to warn you,' she called lightly, laughing again. 'About tonight. Some of the young ones are on duty and there's some plastic mistletoe about. You know what they're like around you. You'd better be on your guard.'

Amused, he lifted his arm in acknowledgement. 'I might borrow some mistletoe myself,' he countered, picturing Maggie's reaction to such a thing. He doubted whether she'd find the joke amusing, but after her performance today he thought he might be entitled to a little light entertainment at her expense. 'You know my bleeper number if you need anything.'

Leaving his jeans and shirt in his locker to retrieve later, he changed into a fresh set of theatre blues for the evening. He had two bleepers to carry—one his normal one, the other an emergency cardiac bleeper that Ian had given him and which he had to carry as part of his role of first on call for ICU—and he clipped one into each pocket of his pants and headed for the unit.

The unit's twelve main beds were arranged in a broad U-shape around the central monitoring unit. There were two other beds off the main ward in side rooms—both had independent air-filtration systems—used for children or when they needed to isolate patients with infectious diseases. At present only eight of the beds were occupied and neither side room and Maggie seemed to have only just started her round because her entourage was only up to the first bed on the left side of the ward, Mr Radcliffe.

Tim, the younger and more chirpy of the unit's two charge nurses, grinned a welcome at him, and the duty physio on for the evening, Steven, and Carol—the staff nurse who was Mr Radcliffe's dedicated carer for the evening—both nodded greetings.

'Will.' Maggie's expression was cool but he could tell from the nervous way that her fingers started to pleat the corner of the day chart she studied that his approach had flustered her—and that pleased him. 'Brian was just explaining that you'd be covering Ian tonight,' she said shakily, 'but, really, there's no need for you to worry about the unit. I'll be here. Why don't you concentrate on your theatre work?'

'Because Theatre's quiet and we're not,' he responded calmly. He greeted the others. 'How does that chest look?' he asked, wanting to see the X-ray he'd ordered when he'd visited Mr Radcliffe earlier with Ian. 'Any improvement?'

'Essentially none since this morning.' Maggie met his mild look neutrally before her eyes darted away again, but her stiffness betrayed her frustration. The X-ray was displayed on a light-backed board at the rear of the main nursing station and they all came with him to study it. 'There just might be a little more fluid here on the right but it's impossible to be sure.'

Will nodded his agreement. He'd admitted Mr Radcliffe ten days previously before his trip to Australia. He'd been in heart failure following a heart attack which had left a large amount of the muscle in the left ventricle of his heart severely damaged. His heart had gone into a form of shock where it was unable to pump efficiently and to maintain a good enough blood pressure to keep his tissues supplied with oxygen.

He was beyond the age group where he could be considered for a heart transplant, even if that treatment had been easily available, and yet he was far too young and active for them to have considered letting nature take its normal course immediately.

He was sedated, paralysed and ventilated to minimise his oxygen requirements and potentially allow time and energy for his heart to recover. Maggie had threaded a special line with a wide balloon on it up through an artery in his leg until it sat just beneath the arch of his aorta. The balloon inflated and deflated automatically and worked as a mechanical pump, helping, among other things, to improve the heart's own blood supply. He had a Swan-Ganz in site as well, monitoring his fluid levels and how well his heart was functioning.

Will lifted the headphones of the mini-stereo set away from Mr Radcliffe's head. It was routine practice in the unit to play local radio stations to every patient to try and keep those who could still hear in touch with real life. 'Mr Radcliffe, hello. It's Dr Saunders again. I'm just going to listen to your chest once more.'

As he replaced the headset he caught a few strains of the music their patient had been listening to, and he sent Carol a weary look. 'If you're a closet rap-music fan then I apologise for this, Mr Radcliffe.' He altered the radio's settings to tune it into a more conventional station. 'But I suspect you'll be happier with this.'

'Carol…?'

'It's only been on that for an hour,' the young, spiky-haired nurse told him with a grin. 'I thought Mr Radcliffe might like it for a change.'

'If you ever end up in here as a patient I'm personally going to prescribe you full-time Verdi.'

'Who's Verdi?'

'My point exactly.' He exchanged understanding smiles with Maggie then bent back to his patient. Using the stethoscope specifically assigned to Mr Radcliffe he quickly checked his heart and lungs, deciding that, despite the ambivalent X-ray findings, his right side definitely sounded more crackly—or fluid-filled—than it had earlier.

He withdrew and stood beside Maggie, aware of the sweet, delicate fragrance of her skin as they checked the day's chart. Mr Radcliffe's medication, aside from the routine cocktail they prescribed for all unit patients—vitamins and drugs designed to reduce the risk of developing stress ulceration within the oesophagus and stomach—was aimed at encouraging the heart to pump more efficiently and at decreasing the amount of work the heart should have to do to keep the kidneys and other organs functioning properly. So far, though, despite intensive treatment, there'd been no improvement.

'Steven mentioned that you altered his dopamine slightly,' Maggie commented, referring to one of the drugs designed to improve the blood supply to the kidneys. 'We've been playing with that most of the week but he's been on haemofiltration for eight days now.' She indicated the small blue and white machine beside the bed. Its blood-filled tubing covered with silver foil, the device filtered the blood in a similar way to dialysis machines and here was being used to manage Mr Radcliffe's kidney failure and to try and control his body's fluid levels. 'We're not going to get any response and his heart rate's gone up.'

Will confirmed that by checking with the monitor above

the bed. 'It was always going to be a juggling act with him,' he said quietly. The increased dose of dopamine might potentially be good for his kidneys but one of its side-effects was to increase the heart rate and that was certainly not good for a failing heart. 'What do you think?' As well as being an intensive care physician, Maggie had specialist training in cardiology and he was happy to go along with whatever she wanted here.

'Let's lower the dose again,' she suggested, exchanging nods with Carol before charting in the drugs section of the day sheet the reduced rate she wanted for the infusion. She sighed. 'Will, you know we're running short of options here. In fact, I'm ready to say that we're out of them. Too much of his heart is too badly damaged. He's not going to respond.'

'Does the family know what's going on?'

'I've spoken with them every day,' she said. Her eyes met his in another brief moment of understanding, and he realised that she knew as well as he did the probable outcome of this case.

It was sad, he acknowledged. It was always sad. But there were times, and she knew it as well as he did, when they no longer had anything to offer. It was a shared knowledge that was never pleasant and, having worked in the past with ICU consultants who tended to deny the inevitability of their lack of success in saving some people, he'd never ceased to be grateful that as clinicians both he and Maggie had the same sort of reasoned response to such things.

They were standing to one side now, away from the bed and out of range of being overheard by Mr Radcliffe or any other patient or visiting relative. She looked up at him solemnly. 'What should we do?'

'Nothing until after Boxing Day,' he said quietly, checking with Tim and Carol to be sure that they were in agreement. 'Give the family Christmas together. Reduce the sedation in the meantime to wake him up a little more and see how we get on. Continue supportive treatment. No active resuscitation if he should arrest again.'

'Agreed.' Maggie's nod mirrored those of the two nurses and Steven.

'How will the family take it?' From before he'd gone away Will remembered that Mr Radcliffe had a large, extended one.

'We've been careful not to be unfairly optimistic from the start,' Tim told him. He looked quickly at Maggie. 'Maggie or Ian and Steven or I have talked to them in detail every day, and his own nurses have been very honest as well. They seem very good at expressing their emotions and they definitely understand that there was only ever a small chance he'd pull through this.'

'They're very religious,' Carol, the other nurse, added, 'particularly his wife and the two oldest sons. They've made it clear that they wouldn't be happy making any decisions themselves. I believe they'll accept the idea of us letting him wake up so we can see what happens.'

Will nodded. There were people who wanted to be consulted about every decision, involving their relative's care, and there were those who wanted to know nothing, and there was every nuance in between. In his experience the ICU nurses were the staff who grew closest to the relatives, and they were invariably the ones best equipped to elicit the family's wishes. 'Good,' he said. 'Then that's what we'll do.'

'I've been dithering these past couple of days, not sure I knew what was the best course to take,' Maggie said. 'Thanks.'

Will looked down at her thoughtfully. 'I've never known you to dither.'

'But, then, of course, you don't know me very well,' she countered, avoiding his eyes. 'You'd be surprised. I dither about a lot of things.'

'Like what?' Intrigued, he wasn't sure he believed her. Carol and Tim, along with their physio, had left them temporarily to assess Mr Radcliffe's half-hourly recordings and Steven had been called away to answer his bleeper so they were briefly alone.

'Like shopping, clothes—even books I want to buy,' she said thinly, still not looking at him but, apparently, after their earlier encounter lacking the courage, for now, to tell him to mind his own business.

'Like shopping?' he echoed. 'What about shopping?'

'About whether I want to buy wholemeal bread or multi-grain,' she answered, the words seeming almost forced from her although she still didn't tell him to go away. 'Like if I prefer bananas or apples. Like deciding between crunchy or smooth peanut butter. We're not all perfect, rational beings, Will. We all dither sometimes. Even you, I imagine, at some stage in your charmed and blessed life must have dithered about something.'

'But not you,' he protested, his mouth quirking at her sarcasm, all the while entranced by the image of the cool, collected woman in front of him standing bewildered in a supermarket aisle. 'Not at work, Maggie. I've never seen you even hesitate about anything.'

'Well, occasionally I do.'

'But—'

'I wanted your advice,' she said coolly, her face still composed and mask-like, although her eyes blazed with a brief flare of heated green. 'Is that good enough for you? I didn't want to change his management without hearing your opinion.'

'That's all you had to say,' he said softly, delighted to

have provoked an emotional response from her so easily. What a difference a week away had made. She'd lowered her guard. He didn't understand how or when or why, but he loved it. The beautiful, *human* woman he'd spied, kicking the grass beneath Jeremy's office, had not been an enchanting figment of his imagination but merely the woman in front of him.

'There's no need for any dramatics,' he teased, sensing that of all things he could have said that would irritate her most. 'That's fine. I'm happy to offer advice. That's what I'm here for.'

'What you should be here for is the ward round,' she announced, her glorious eyes frankly hostile, before she moved away towards Tim who'd come back. 'Unless you've any objections, I suggest we see Mrs Adams next.'

'No objections at all,' he said lightly, going with her. 'Ian mentioned her briefly but you'll have to fill me in. When did she come in? Yesterday?'

'Early hours of Tuesday morning,' her nurse corrected. 'Drunk driver.'

'The other driver, not her,' Maggie said quietly. 'It was a head-on impact, slightly angled from the right. The other driver was killed.' She started with Mrs Adams's bandaged head. 'Right parietal fracture,' she said, referring to a type of skull fracture. 'The neurosurgeons were happy and the CT scan at the time showed only very minimal swelling, but we kept her sedated and ventilated to control her gases.'

Will nodded. The amount of brain swelling that developed following an injury was influenced by the amount of carbon dioxide in the blood and the level of blood flow to the brain. By controlling those things via ventilation it was possible to minimise swelling.

'CT scan this morning was essentially normal but because of her lungs we haven't attempted to wake her.'

Maggie moved on to indicate the chest drain, coming out of the bandaged right side of Mrs Adams's chest. The fluid in the bottom of the bottle was blood-stained and Maggie confirmed the type of lung injury. 'Right pulmonary contusions with dense consolidation at the base of the lung, which we assume is an aspiration pneumonia from the time of her injury. Also, there're signs of more widespread changes, just starting this afternoon.'

She moved slightly so he could see the ventilator readings her arm had been concealing, as well as the oxygen measurement coming from a small clip on Mrs Adams's left ear. 'Saturations have dropped despite increasing her oxygen.'

'Ninety-one.' He read the figure from the ear monitor. 'Not too bad.'

'Yet. That's on sixty-eight per cent oxygen as well as eight centimetres PEEP.' PEEP was a type of positive pressure ventilation which held the lungs more fully inflated than normal. It was risky, like here, where there was a lung injury, and he knew that the fact that Maggie was using it signified her high level of concern about Mrs Adams's oxygen levels. 'We're covering the pneumonia with antibiotics, of course.'

'But you think this is ARDS?'

'Have you seen the latest chest X-ray?'

He shook his head and they went to the board where he inspected the serial films gravely. As well as the pneumonia at the right base, there were the beginnings of widespread changes consistent with ARDS. Adult Respiratory Distress Syndrome, sometimes called shock lung, was a serious, potentially fatal and not well-understood complication of many injuries and diseases and led to the lungs filling with fluid.

'We had a look down this afternoon with the bronchoscope and took washings and samples of the infection,' Maggie told him. 'We should have something specific through tonight on which bugs are the problem on the right.'

They went back to the bed and Maggie indicated further down Mrs Adams's body. 'Ruptured spleen, requiring nine units of blood and clotting factors plus platelets to resuscitate, but no further signs of trouble there. Platelet count today within normal limits.' She lifted back the sheet so that he could see the patient's surgical wound, then replaced it.

'Open fracture right femur, closed left femur,' Maggie continued, and he nodded. The orthopods had obviously been busy—the right femur was externally pinned and open while the left leg was encased in a cast.

'Dr Saunders?' Hine, the nurse looking after Mrs Adams, looked a little hesitant. 'This drip has tissued on this side and I've tried three times but I haven't been able to get another one in. It's her only peripheral line and we're just using it for her antibiotics, but we're late for the six o'clock doses. We wouldn't normally ask you but since Ian's not here…'

'I couldn't find a vein either,' Steven said sheepishly. 'Sorry.'

Maggie said, 'It's all right. She's not easy. That's fine. I'll do it as soon as we finish the round.'

'No, you won't.' Will met Maggie's sharp look blandly. He might be the director of the unit, but for tonight he was the acting junior doctor on call and he hadn't taken on the task with the intention of offloading his duties onto Maggie. 'You continue here. I'll organise this.'

Hine already had a drip trolley ready for him. 'Pink all right?' She indicated the differently coloured cannulas the unit carried.

'Fine.' While Maggie discussed the chart and talked about her patient's management with the charge nurse and Steven, Will washed his hands, applied a tourniquet to Mrs Adams's bruised arm, swabbed her skin, then searched for a suitable vein.

'No wonder you and Steven had problems,' he said to Hine, changing the tourniquet to Mrs Adams's other arm when he failed to find a good vessel on the right. He sent her a quick, sympathetic smile. 'This is quite difficult.'

He could just feel a slight bounce in texture, suggesting a vein along the outside of her forearm, and he unscrewed the cannula and swiftly inserted it, all the while talking gently to their unconscious patient and explaining what he was doing in case she could hear him.

Hine was ready with the dressing and he stood back to let her finish, then continued with the others to their next patient.

They didn't finish until almost seven-thirty, the round having taken longer than usual, but because of his time away Will had let Maggie lead, enjoying her thorough and systematic approach to every case.

'Tea and gingernuts?' Prue, one of the other senior nurses on for the unit, beamed at them when they returned to the monitoring station. She waggled her eyebrows wickedly. 'Or, since I'm merely the floating nurse tonight, as a special Christmas treat—if you can give me a few minutes to finish some paperwork—I could bring you some of my famous brandy chocolate truffles.'

'Truffles, please.' Not merely famous, Prue's brandy truffles were legendary. Will had fond memories of them from years earlier when he'd been a registrar in Wellington's main ICU and Prue had been a staff nurse there. 'Finish whatever you have to finish,' he said. 'We'll wait in the staffroom.'

'I just need to make a phone call,' Steven said, excusing himself. 'I'll catch up with you in a few minutes.'

As the other doctor moved away Maggie made a small dissenting murmur herself and checked her watch pointedly. Before she could say anything Will took her arm and turned her immediately stiff but surprisingly unresisting form around. 'We'll get the drinks,' he told Prue, pushing Maggie in front of him. 'You bring the truffles.'

Maggie started to protest, but he hushed her. 'You haven't lived till you've tried one of Prue's truffles,' he told her firmly. 'Whatever it is, it can wait.'

'I haven't got a sweet tooth,' she argued. 'I hardly ever eat chocolate. And I'd like to go back to Snell—'

'These truffles will change your mind about chocolate.' He closed the door to contain her. 'And I'll come with you to Obstetrics as soon as we've had coffee. Sit. If they need us urgently they'll bleep one of us.'

When she sat, obviously still reluctant but not actually arguing, he put the water on to boil. In the unit the only signs of Christmas had been one wan plastic holly garland and a tiny strip of tinsel around Tim's name badge. Here, though, the great stack of decorations in the corner of the room suggested that the nurses had big plans for the evening. 'Looks like the nurses are turning militant.'

'Wonderful, isn't it?' She sent him a small smile. 'They're waiting until they think it's safe to put them up. Personally, I think they were safe yesterday. I doubt if the bigwig who wrote that disgusting memo bothered to come in to work on Christmas Eve.'

'Probably sunning himself in Fiji,' Will agreed, spooning instant coffee into mugs.

'More likely somewhere much more expensive and far away,' she argued. 'The Bahamas or Brazil. My guess is we won't see him around here until the end of January.'

'Maggie, such cynicism.' But he laughed, pleased that their views on such things corresponded. 'You shock me.'

'I doubt it,' she said crisply.

'You're probably right.' The water had now boiled and he poured it, then added milk to her coffee and handed it to her. He put a teaspoon of sugar into Prue's mug, milk and sugar into Steven's and left his own black. 'Today I might just be getting used to being shocked by you.'

Her expression didn't change but she drew herself up a little and he had the impression that she was tensing inside. 'Will, I've already said I'm sorry—'

'Don't.' He lifted his free hand. 'It's all right,' he said easily. 'Relax. I was teasing. I accept your apology.'

'You know that if I'd thought about it—'

'If *I'd* thought about it I'd have realised that I've probably given you every reason to suspect such a thing,' he interrupted. 'It's not as if I've ever gone out of my way to conceal what I want.'

'No.' The word came out huskily. Definitely paler now, she was staring down into her coffee, refusing to met his eyes. He felt guilty but it was so rare for them to communicate in any way but obliquely that he couldn't stop himself continuing.

'All you've ever had to say is no.'

'I've said no.' Her head still firmly lowered, she didn't look at him. 'Lots of times.'

'You haven't,' he said gently. And it was true. It was the irony that had driven him crazy and it was the reason her deliberate distancing of herself infuriated him so much. He was experienced enough to know when a woman was aware of him and Maggie had always been that.

'You've never told me no,' he said. 'You've said things like, ''Not today'' and ''Not this weekend'', ''I don't like boats'' and ''No, I want to work over the break and I don't want to go away''. That's all, Maggie. You've never said, ''No, Will, I'm not interested''. You've never said, ''I'll never be interested''. You've never said, ''Please don't ask me again''.'

'Perhaps I didn't expect you to be so persistent.'

'Bad luck,' he said flatly. 'I am.'

'You're stubborn.'

'When I know what I want,' he agreed, his focus entirely on the silky crown of her lowered head as he willed her to look at him.

'Don't.' She pushed her barely touched coffee away and stood, turning from him so that he still couldn't see her expression. 'You're not being fair. You're putting me in a very difficult position.'

'What do you mean, I'm not being fair?' he asked wearily. Then he stopped, suddenly realising, abruptly sickened by the thought of what she might be implying. 'You mean because I'm your boss?' he demanded.

'Of course not,' she said immediately, spinning around, her eyes wide and startled enough to relax him at least a little. 'No, you've always been completely professional, I know that. I don't... No, this has nothing to do with work.'

'Thank God for that,' he breathed.

'But that doesn't mean I understand why you still...' She tailed off. 'Will, I've never encouraged you. Not once. But you keep asking. I've never understood why.'

'Even you cannot be that naïve,' he growled, putting his own coffee aside and leaning back against the wall with his hands in the pockets of his blues. 'Come on, Maggie. Be rational. Since when have men ever needed any encouragement?'

'You're a very attractive man,' she said shakily, now at the window with her back to him, her body held achingly taut. 'You're a very attractive, *sexy* man.' He didn't move.

The words did nothing for him—the sentiment was irrelevant unless it influenced the way she responded now. 'There are many women around here who'd be more than happy—'

'I don't want *many* women,' he said harshly, the stupidity of her words making him want to tear away the veils she was using to hide herself from him. 'I don't want other women, Maggie. You know that. We both know that. I want you.'

CHAPTER FOUR

MAGGIE squeezed her eyes shut so tightly that her lids ached. 'Please don't say things like that,' she said finally, feeling as if she had to force the words out from between her gritted teeth.

'Why shouldn't I when we both know it's the truth?'

'I don't want to hear it.'

'So what am I supposed to do?' Will demanded. 'Spend another eleven months pretending there's nothing going on here? And then how long? Another year? Another ten? For God's sake, Maggie! How long are you going to deny this?'

'There's nothing to deny,' she rasped. 'This is all in your imagination—'

'I'm imagining nothing.' His voice was shockingly raw, and she found herself reaching out blindly to grab at the metal of the window-frame in some sort of feeble attempt to secure herself, but her senses told her that he hadn't moved, hadn't come anywhere near her.

'None of this is one-sided—it's too strong for that. All I want to know is why not? You're not involved with anyone. Is it your ex-husband? Jeremy said that in your interviews you sounded keen to leave Britain. He said he thought your divorce might have had something to do with that because someone told him that your husband had worked at the same hospital. Did you want to leave because you were frightened of him? Did he...hurt you?'

'No.' It was true, at least it was in the physical sense he meant, and the fact that he was so wrong restored a little of her internal composure. Slowly she opened the eyes she'd still been holding squeezed shut, blinking quickly to

59

relieve the tiny spasms the relief provoked in the small muscles around her eyes. 'We parted...amiably.'

'Then there's something else. Has someone else hurt you? A stranger, perhaps? Another lover?'

'You're becoming melodramatic.' Smoothing her features carefully, she allowed herself to turn and meet his demanding blue gaze with a determined calmness she was nowhere near feeling. 'Obviously it's never occurred to you that, however strongly you might feel, I'm simply not interested.'

'No, that has never occurred to me,' he said flatly, what he thought of her remark immediately plain from the scathing look he sent her. 'Believe it or not, I have a little more experience than that.'

She believed it. Inwardly, perhaps, she'd pretended to herself that he'd never guess, but of course she'd known all along that he knew. 'All right,' she conceded, electing to bluff it out rather than become emotional. 'Since you're so determined to hear the complete truth. You're right, of course. There's no point in trying to hide that.'

The air between them seemed suddenly electrified. 'Tell me how I'm right,' he urged softly. 'Tell me how exactly.'

'There's nothing to be gained by being coy about this,' Maggie said thickly. 'You're obviously used to having this effect on women.' She swallowed heavily, her eyes caught, hypnotised almost by the compelling warmth of his gaze. He was five yards away from her, not touching her, yet his eyes burned her. The room seemed almost to hum.

'Of course you're right,' she admitted huskily. 'The unfortunate fact is that, regardless of how much I try to control it, I do find myself...reacting to you. There is something between us. I do find myself attracted to you in a...sexual way.'

The sudden blaring emergency shrill of Will's bleeper shattered the mood, making her jump, and at the same moment Prue shoved open the staffroom door, followed closely by Steven.

'No time for truffles—sorry,' the nurse apologised. 'Snell Ward just called,' she hissed to Maggie, lowering her voice as if she was worried about drowning out the voice issuing from Will's bleeper. 'They're doing an emergency Caesarean on the woman you told us about. They wanted to warn us about her coming here afterwards.'

Maggie saw Will shove his bleeper back into the pocket of his pants. 'They need help with the anaesthetic,' he said, making for the corridor. 'She's fitting. Steven, you should come and see this.'

'What about the baby?' Prue asked Maggie, when the two other doctors had left. 'Should we prepare for that?'

'Just in case,' Maggie agreed automatically, still shaking from the encounter with Will even though he was gone. But the puzzled look the nurse gave her brought her attention back. 'Yes, you'd better,' she said, more firmly now, suspecting that it would be overly optimistic to hope that the baby would be well enough to be managed in the special care baby unit in the obstetric block.

It was an eight-bedded unit, ideal for mildly premature infants and those with jaundice or needing monitoring, it wasn't meant for critically ill babies. Those needing ventilation—and this baby was so young he or she would, especially since the steroids the mother would have been given to try and mature his or her lungs would hardly have had enough time to work yet—were usually stabilised first either in Theatres or temporarily in ICU, then transferred by road or by helicopter to the specialist neonatal unit at Wellington's main hospital in Newtown, or further afield if beds were full.

It wasn't the ideal arrangement. They had equipment and two single beds which could be adapted for children but they weren't designed for managing babies, certainly not very premature babies, and the staff were consequently not very experienced at looking after them. But until funds became available for the extra dedicated paediatric intensive care beds the country needed it was the best they could manage. 'If they send the baby, he or she will already be in an incubator from Theatres,' she added.

'The supervisor's arranging for one of the SCBU nurses to come to us just in case,' Prue informed her. 'Most of them have spent time in Wellington. They know what they're doing.'

They were back in the unit now and Hine, the nurse looking after Mrs Adams, called for her. 'Maggie, saturations are falling,' she said, referring to the oxygen levels in their patient's blood. 'I've pushed her PEEP up to ten,' she added, 'plus I've had to put her oxygen up to seventy per cent.'

She handed Maggie a small print-out of the latest results. Mrs Adams had an arterial line in place at her wrist and the nurses took blood samples from it every half-hour and tested them in a machine kept on the unit which accurately measured the concentrations of the blood gases. Maggie ran her eye down the readings, comparing them to the records Hine had charted over the course of the day.

'Her blood pressure's dropped,' Hine added, looking at the monitor which displayed the results coming from the same arterial line.

'I'll check her chest again.' Maggie nodded her thanks when the nurse helped to pull the screens around the bed. 'Are you and the physio still getting much up from the tube?'

'Not since this morning.' Hine showed her the latest sample she'd taken during routine suctioning of Mrs Adams's ET tube—the tube in her throat connecting her to her ventilator.

The nurse helped hold Mrs Adams forward so that

Maggie could listen to all areas of her chest. There was still considerable clinical infection at the base of the injured lung but the opposite side now sounded more crackly than it had even an hour earlier. 'Another chest X-ray,' she ordered. 'Repeat the white cell count and a general screen, including clotting. Do blood cultures, line cultures, urine, take down the wound dressings so we can check them and do the usual routine swabs. I'll call Microbiology and see if any results are through yet.'

She touched her patient's shoulder reassuringly and, as she did routinely, explained what they'd be doing on the off chance that she could hear anything they'd been saying.

Mrs Adams's husband was hovering anxiously outside the screens. 'Is there another problem, Dr Miller? Is it her temperature again?'

'I think it's probably the chest problem we talked about earlier,' Maggie said gently. 'The little monitor on her ear and the latest blood test show that we're not getting as much oxygen as we'd like into her blood. The infection might be getting worse but her lungs also aren't working as well as they were this morning. Hine's going to organise for another chest X-ray and we'll go from there.'

'She's had an X-ray already today.'

'We still need to check again to be sure.'

'Remember yesterday you thought there might be a problem from the breathing machine?' he said hesitantly. 'Could it be that again?'

'It's a very small possibility,' she said slowly, 'but not likely.' When Mrs Adams's saturations had dropped the day before Maggie had explained that they'd been worried about the possibility that ventilation had damaged the lung, although, in fact, what had happened was that Mrs Adams had developed an infection.

Because they were using positive pressure ventilation, where oxygen was driven into the lungs—the best way of

ensuring that air reached every corner of the lungs and kept
them well inflated—there was a possibility that an air leak
could occur through some of the damaged lung tissue on
her right side. But if the air leak had occurred, air would
by now have been bubbling out under the water in the chest
drain on that side, and that wasn't happening.

'But whatever is wrong should show on the X-ray,' Mr
Adams said earnestly.

'It should. The X-ray will also give us information about
the infection and whether that's spreading and causing her
problems now, or it will tell us if it's the shocked lung
problem, getting worse. It also shows us that all our lines
are in the right place and general things like that.'

'I understand.' He spoke quietly. 'Thank you. Will you
tell me what you see?'

'Of course.' She touched his arm reassuringly. Not a big
man, and considerably older than his wife, he'd grown no-
ticeably frailer, she thought, over the past few days.
'Remember the canteen closes at eight and then after that
there's only the machine. Have you had some supper?'

'I'll find something later.' He took his wife's fingers in
his. 'Thank you, Dr Miller.'

She bleeped Microbiology. 'Definitely an awful mixture,' the technician told her cheerfully, detailing the various different types of bacteria he'd been able to isolate from
the specimens she'd sent him earlier that day. 'Any chance
she's aspirated?'

'It's very likely,' Maggie told him unhappily. 'What
about sensitivities?'

'Won't be through until tomorrow,' he said, and she nodded, not surprised. It usually took another day to find out
which antibiotics the isolated bacteria were most sensitive
to.

'We're already covering for everything they're likely to
find,' Maggie explained to Hine, 'so the actual sensitivities

shouldn't make much difference, but at least we'll know for sure what we're dealing with.'

'The radiographer's coming up now to do the chest X-ray,' Hine told her. 'I've already sent the blood off.'

'Maggie, is there anything special I should get ready for our obstetrics lady?' Prue hurried across. 'What do you prefer to use in case she fits again? Phenytoin?'

'Depends what Will's giving her now,' Maggie told her. 'He'll have started either magnesium sulphate or phenytoin in Theatres and we'll simply continue whichever one he's used. I suspect he probably prefers mag. sulph.'

The telephone beside Maggie chimed. It was the haematology technician, calling back with Mrs Adams's blood results.

'Haemoglobin 110,' she said, and Maggie wrote the figures in a notebook kept by the phone for that specific purpose. 'White cell count, twenty-eight point six.' She detailed the breakdown of the results which showed that the predominant cell was the one which specialised in fighting bacterial infections. Platelets 150.'

'Her white count's almost doubled since this morning,' Maggie told Hine wearily. 'This is not turning into a very good Christmas Eve.'

'Christmas will never be good in ICU,' Hine said dully. 'Never. Not with all the car accidents. Touch wood, we haven't had our usual run of overdoses yet.'

Will came back to the unit an hour later with their new obstetric patient. Still anaesthetised, Mrs Everett looked stable from where Maggie stood, but Will's eyes met hers briefly but unreadably while an orderly and Prue wheeled the bed towards the one Prue had prepared.

Refusing to allow their earlier encounter to impair her professional behaviour towards Will, Maggie went to help him and Steven and the nurses, controlling Linda Everett's feet while they transferred her from the bed she must have had on Snell onto one of their own beds with its warmed-air mattress.

'We heard the helicopter,' she said in an undertone once their patient was settled and they'd moved away. She still found herself not quite able to meet Will's gaze. 'How's the baby?'

'Distressed. Apgars two and five,' he said quietly, referring to the scoring system used to rate the way babies were breathing and reacting at birth. Taken at one minute and five minutes after delivery, the normal later level was ten so the low result meant that the baby was very unwell. 'There's a spare bed in Neonates in Wellington,' he added efficiently. 'The paeds reg. has taken him straight in to it.'

'What about here?' Maggie hooked up the bag of dextrose they'd lowered for the transfer onto the pole at the head of the air-bed.

'Three seizures pre op,' Will told her. 'She had a dose of i.v. diazepam and loading with mag. sulph.' He indicated the blue infusion pump beside him. 'That's going at one gram in twenty-four hours. If she fits again we'll give another two grams i.v.'

'But with the anaesthetic...' Steven looked up '...how will we know if she's fitting?'

'Alarms will start going off,' she heard Will explain. 'If she convulses the infusions will back up and the machine won't be able to ventilate her meaning we'll have to switch to bagging manually.'

Maggie swapped Theatre's pulse oximeter, the machine they used to record blood oxygen saturation levels, for one of the unit's machines, then she clipped its end over their patient's left little finger. 'How's her blood pressure been?'

'Brittle.' Will opened each of Mrs Everett's eyes in turn and shone his torch into her pupils. 'She was very restless before I put her under. I want a CT scan of her head to exclude haemorrhage and to check how swollen her brain is, before making any attempt to wake her up. In the meantime, we'll keep her hyperventilated. I've put out a call for the radiologist on call.'

'What do you want me to do?'

'See what's wrong with that radial artery line,' Will instructed, nodding to their patient's right arm, busy now himself at the anaesthetic machine. The small pump through which the line was fed was bleeping softly. 'I've only just put it in. The tubing probably kinked when we were transferring.'

As he'd predicted, she discovered that the only problem was a small kink in the line connecting the cannula to the pressure sensor and to the heparinised saline slowly being dripped through it to keep it patent. She gently flushed the cannula, reprogrammed the pump, then took a small sample of blood for testing, before starting the pump again and triggering the device which would monitor the arterial blood pressure via the line.

'Gases are good,' she told him, when she came back a few seconds later. She passed him the print-out of the results, warming slightly at the quick, appreciative smile he sent her.

His bleeper shrilled but his hands were busy and he moved himself so that she could gingerly extract the device from his hip pocket. She pressed the button to activate the voice message. 'Dr Saunders,' the static-distorted voice said, 'you have an outside call. Dr Saunders, outside call.'

'Want me to get it?'

'Please.' Preoccupied with his task, his smile now was brief and impersonal. 'It could be our radiologist, calling back.'

But when Maggie took the call on the main ICU extension she discovered that it was his mother, calling, she said, from Auckland. George Barnes, the obstetrician looking after Mrs Adams, had come into the unit, his registrar in tow, and he'd gone straight to her bed, obviously consulting with Will. Maggie knew her colleague wouldn't want to be interrupted.

'I'm sorry, but he's busy just now,' she said loudly, speaking clearly so that his mother would be able to hear her over what sounded like a very noisy party in the background. 'Shall I ask him to call you back?'

'Not to worry, dear,' the friendly voice promptly roared back—so loudly that Maggie had to hold the receiver away from her ear. 'We're just about to go off carol singing,' his mother shouted, sounding out each word slowly and individually. 'He won't take any notice but tell him not to work too hard.'

Maggie came back gingerly to the receiver. 'I will.'

'We thought we'd surprise Will with this but here's a little treat for you instead.' His mother was still shouting but then in a lower voice, presumably to the people around her—and perhaps not meant for her to hear—Maggie heard her hiss, 'Sing up, all of you, as loud as you can. Will's too busy, poor boy. Get closer to me. There's a very nice friend of his here but she's terribly deaf.'

Maggie knew that it was a Christmas carol because she vaguely recognised the melody, and it seemed that his mother, at least, could hold a tune and she was obviously closest to the telephone. Even if she hadn't had to hold the receiver six inches from her ear to muffle the collective roar, the words, aside from the odd 'Merry Christmas' they were wishing her, were unintelligible.

At some stage during the performance Will looked up from his discussion with the obstetrician, his brow creasing as he saw she was still on the phone. 'What?' he mouthed, but she shook her head, waving to tell him that there was nothing to worry about.

'Well, dear?' His mother was back, roaring again. 'What did you think?'

'I'm stunned,' Maggie said truthfully. 'Thank you.'

'You're welcome.' The older woman sounded thrilled. 'She says we're stunning,' she hissed. Maggie assumed she was talking to the group around her again because there were prompt sounds of general agreement. 'Have a lovely Christmas, dear,' Will's mother finished. 'Tell Will we'll all call him again tomorrow. Goodbye.'

'Maggie, Microbiology say they've found white cells and gram-negative rods in Mrs Adams's urine.' Hine had taken a call on another line while Maggie had been talking with Will's mother and now she came up as soon as Maggie was finished.

'When are you doing the next gentamicin level?' Maggie wondered if they needed to increase the dose of the powerful antibiotic. Gram-negative rods suggested that the type of bacteria infecting the urine were ones which gentamicin would probably treat, and they had already prescribed it, along with several others. But it was a toxic drug, and as Mrs Adams's kidneys were already not functioning as well as normal they had to monitor closely the concentration of gentamicin in her blood to be sure that they were giving the optimal dose.

'Pre and post the nine o'clock dose tonight,' Hine answered, checking the clock on the wall behind Maggie as Maggie herself spun to study it. 'Another thirty minutes.'

'Trouble?'

Will's quiet enquiry brought her back round again, and she briefly explained what had been happening with Mrs Adams. 'Chest X-ray shows worsening ARDS, ' she told him. 'Her latest urine's infected—it was clear yesterday—and we've had to up her oxygen and PEEP again. We're keeping her dry so her renal function's dropping off, but we've kept her on gentamicin for now. Hine's just about to take levels.' She swung the notebook around so he could see the actual laboratory results.

He came with her to the bed. 'Mr Adams, this is Dr Saunders, the director of the unit,' Maggie explained, introducing Will to Mrs Adams's husband, who hadn't moved from his wife's bedside since Maggie had given him the bad news about the chest X-ray.

Will shook the older man's hand. 'We'll only be a few minutes,' he told him. 'You're welcome to stay.'

'I think I'll go and get a cup of tea.' Mr Adams's hesitant gaze sought out Maggie. 'If that's all right.'

Maggie nodded. 'Of course it is.'

They waited until he was out of the unit, before swiftly hauling the screens around the bed. Will went to the chart while Hine and Maggie pulled back the sheet which covered the patient. Maggie crouched to inspect the hourly urine-collecting reservoir attached to the catheter, lifting the tubing so the contents would flow into the dish. 'Twenty mils,' she told Hine. 'Is that for the half-hour?'

'Thirty-five minutes,' the staff nurse told her, nodding acknowledgement of the figure.

As Maggie had done earlier, Will swiftly examined Mrs Adams. 'Cultures from the lines?'

'From everywhere,' Hine confirmed.

'I've started full anti-staph cover,' Maggie added, meaning she'd added an antibiotic specifically aimed at killing the type of bacteria which commonly infected intravenous lines.

'Her abdomen's soft,' Will said quietly. 'Wound's clean. Good bowel sounds. Unlikely that we're dealing with an infection here.' He passed the stethoscope he'd been using back to Hine, who slung it around part of the metal bedhead. 'How long have the naso-gastric feeds been going?'

'Started yesterday,' Hine told him. 'We've built up slowly and she's now almost up to full strength.'

'We didn't consider intravenous feeding.' Maggie saw that he was studying the contents of the plastic bottle that contained Mrs Adams's dietary requirements. 'According to the surgeons, the only abdominal injury was the spleen—and her bowel wasn't damaged at all. We haven't had any problems with it.'

He'd dulled the lights above the bed and now he took the ophthalmoscope Maggie passed him. He looked though its lens then homed in on Mrs Adams's right eye, holding it open gently with two fingers. 'Have the neurosurgeons been back to review her?'

'This afternoon,' she confirmed. The area's neurosurgical team's main unit was at Wellington hospital but the surgeons did regular rounds at both sites. 'They were confident there's nothing to worry about on their side of things.'

'I agree,' Will said, withdrawing once he'd finished his examination. 'In fact, right now her head injury's the last of her problems.' The set of his mouth was grim. 'Mr Adams…?'

'I'll speak to him as soon as we've finished,' she answered in an undertone.

He came to stand with her back at the chart. 'Let's pull all this together,' he said quietly. 'We've two confirmed foci of infection—chest and urine.'

'Treating for both,' Maggie noted.

'Rapidly deteriorating renal function…' he glanced up at the readings coming from the Ganz '…rising potassium, deteriorating respiratory and cardiac function. Fluid balance…' he traced a finger down the chart where the numbers Hine had written in red constituted the cumulative volume for the day '…less than optimal. We've got to get rid of more of that fluid. Oxygenation…' he looked at the saturation monitor '…maintained, but only with an increase in the inspired concentration up to seventy-five per cent and PEEP at ten centimetres.'

'Maintained at the moment,' Maggie said softly, knowing, from the seriousness of his expression, that he shared her concern.

If they had to they could push the amount of oxygen up to one hundred per cent—almost five times the normal amount in the air—but that was something they preferred to avoid. ARDS carried a high mortality, but if the patient survived, after having breathed oxygen concentrations above eighty per cent, she was at risk of permanent lung damage from oxygen toxicity alone.

'Let's take a litre and a half of fluid off her to start and add in adrenaline and dopamine,' Will instructed, reaching for the chart. 'Since the head injury's stable we'll try moving her over onto her front. We'll add in nitric oxide. Hine, while you organise the infusions I'll do the gas, then we'll turn her over. Maggie, you'd better put Mr Adams in the picture.'

She found him in the relatives' room. The television was broadcasting what looked like a carol service in a cathedral somewhere but he didn't seem to be watching, his eyes instead fixed on the steaming mug he clutched.

His alarmed gaze flew to her when she came in and she came to sit beside him. 'Things aren't getting any better,' she said gently. 'Dr Saunders wants to start very intensive treatment now and I agree with him that it's necessary.'

'Intensive treatment?' he echoed. 'More antibiotics?'

'Some special drugs for her breathing and for her heart. With ARDS, for reasons we don't completely understand, the blood vessels in the lungs become leaky,' she said slowly. 'When that happens fluid flows out of them into the lungs themselves and that prevents them absorbing oxygen properly. We have to force oxygen in as well as trying to dry out the lungs, but it gets complicated because when we do that the heart and circulation and kidneys sometimes don't work as well as normal. The drugs we'll be giving her support the heart and help make sure that all the organs get a good blood supply.'

'I know Hine's been worried about her kidneys,' he said rawly. 'She keeps measuring Barbara's urine all the time. We've got a nephew on dialysis...'

'We're giving her something to try and prevent permanent kidney damage,' Maggie told him, 'but for now she's going to need a sort of mini-dialysis we use here where we take blood from a big vein and put it though filters so we can remove fluid from her system as well as toxins. But she should only need that short term,' she added gently. 'It's not the same thing as being on dialysis for years, like your nephew. Is he waiting for a transplant?'

'Five years now,' he said, nodding sadly. 'One to ten, Dr Miller. Yesterday you said five and a half. How bad is she tonight?'

'If ten is the worst and one is either one of us, I would say...seven,' she said gently. She didn't like scales like that but they seemed to help people come to terms with what was happening.

'I understand.' He nodded his head weakly. 'Thank you.'

She squeezed his hand. 'We're also going to turn her onto her front. She'll have special cushions under her shoulders and her head will be turned to one side but, don't worry, that's what we want. We'll keep turning her that way every few hours. Lying like that seems to help get more oxygen into people's lungs.'

'Shall I wait here?'

'Come through now. You won't be in the way.'

Will was at the nursing station, writing in Mrs Adams's notes, but he looked up when she came towards him and his eyes met hers with a watchful speculation that immediately brought back their earlier conversation in the staff-room and made her stiffen. 'It's going to take a while to set up for haemofiltration,' he said quietly. 'It's after nine.

Steven's gone back to his flat to get some dinner. Have you eaten?'

When she shook her head he came out from behind the station. 'Then let's go.' Disturbingly his arm went across her back and he steered her towards the unit's main door. 'I called the canteen staff from Theatres. They promised to put something aside for us.'

'I'm not hungry,' she protested.

'That doesn't matter.' Obviously understanding the reasons for her attempt at resistance, his regard was knowing. He tugged her forward and, reluctant to cause a scene, she let him.

'If you're really not hungry you can just sit with me and keep me company,' he said softly. 'Besides, we need to talk.'

CHAPTER FIVE

CLEARLY the thought of talking about anything with Will left Maggie unimpressed, but he brushed aside her string of excuses, amused by her apparent determination not to spend time with him but pleased that she didn't actually physically try to leave him.

Even as he punched out the security code which would give them access to the area she was still protesting. 'Will, I really couldn't manage anything big. It's too late. I'll just get a sandwich from the machine.'

'There's a machine inside,' he said calmly, opening the door. 'Relax, Maggie. I'm not going to force-feed you.'

She blinked at that, and his mouth quirked. Obviously he'd been right to assume that it was the eating together, rather than what she ate, which was giving her the problem.

Once inside the deserted, gloomy interior—the only lights came from two brightly lit display cabinets containing assorted cans of soft drinks—she fell silent. She didn't try to leave but she didn't come with him behind the counters to the kitchen.

He found the meals where the catering supervisor had told him he would—on a stainless-steel shelf beside one of the ovens. There were two trays and each held a lid-covered plate. 'There's roast lamb or some sort of noodle and chicken thing,' he called. 'Which would you prefer?'

'Chicken.' He heard the sound of money dropping into the drinks machine and when he carried the trays out from behind the counters he saw she'd bought them each a lemon and Paeroa.

Once he was seated he opened one can and took several

thirsty swallows, enjoying the coldness of the sparkling liquid. He saw that she drank her own equally appreciatively and he smiled. 'So your time in New Zealand's given you a taste for our lemon and Paeroa?'

'Definitely.' She studied the can with a faint frown. 'I don't usually enjoy sweet drinks but this is very nice. What exactly is Paeroa?'

'It's a place. A little town up north,' he told her, uncovering his meal. 'At the base of the Coromandel Peninsula. Have you made it up that far yet?'

She shook her head. 'All I've had is two hours in Auckland airport before I flew down here the first time I arrived.' She tasted her food, the delicate movements drawing his attention to the enticing curve of her mouth. 'And, of course, I went back to England to see my mother for this year's holiday so I haven't even made it to Rotorua yet, although it's high on my agenda.'

'One of my brothers has a holiday home just out of town,' he told her. Lance's bach was on Lake Rotoiti in a beautiful spot for fishing and tramping, a short drive from Rotorua's most active thermal sites. It was an ideal base for anyone wanting to see the area's dramatic attractions, and as Lance's job kept him in Auckland pretty much most of the year he was always more than happy for someone else to take advantage of the place. 'Let me know when you want to go.' But then he stopped, eyeing her sudden stiffness impatiently. 'That didn't mean anything,' he said roughly, laying down his knife and fork.

'I didn't say I thought it did,' she answered tightly, not taking her eyes off her food. The silence stretched even though he could feel her awareness of him with every cell in his body.

'You don't have to *say* anything,' he burst out finally, frustration flooding him. He shoved his tray away, his appetite abruptly gone. 'Maggie, why are you still playing games? I thought we'd achieved something earlier.'

'I don't see what.' Coolly, very coolly—so coolly it just about drove him mad—those glorious green eyes lifted to his in apparent indifference to his ire.

'You admitted you felt something,' he grated.

'All I admitted was that I found you sexually attractive.' Her face was a mask, an infuriatingly and maddeningly calm mask. 'I fail to see how that changes anything. You made it perfectly clear that you'd already guessed how I felt. But...' He saw her chest lift slightly as if she was taking a deep breath, but her eyes didn't shift from his, not for a second. 'But that doesn't mean anything's changed,' she continued crisply.

'You might think that sex is the greatest invention in history but I'm afraid that doesn't mean we all share your enthusiasm. I'm not interested in becoming involved with you. As far as I'm concerned, the fantasy's a lot more fun than the reality and I'm sticking with that.'

'Fantasy?' Her revelations stunned him but it was that word that held him spellbound. 'You mean... Have you fantasised...about me?'

'Occasionally.'

His mouth was so dry it hurt. 'Doing...doing what?'

Her gaze faltered. 'Will, this...this is too personal,' she said quickly. She looked down at her dinner. 'Please, just accept that I'm not comfortable discussing this and I'm really not interested in pursuing anything...physical with you.'

He swallowed heavily. 'Maggie, you can't spend your life in your own head. At some time you've got to come out and live.'

Very stiffly she said, 'I'm living perfectly happily, thank you.'

'How can you say that? You're missing so much—'

'The only thing I'm missing out on is *sex*,' she said scathingly, her eyes flicking briefly across his rigid face. 'I don't see that as a sacrifice.'

He felt sick at the thought of what her ex-husband might have done to her. 'Sex is one of the greatest things in the world. With the right partner—'

Her head came up sharply, her eyes narrowed green icicles across his face. 'I'm not frigid.'

He froze. 'I didn't say you—'

'It's obviously what you're thinking.'

'All right, I was.' He was prepared to concede that. 'That's not so unreasonable. You've just sat there as calmly as anything and told me you prefer fantasy to love-making. Of course I'm going to worry about that.'

'I think sex is fine. In fact, I think that at times it's quite enjoyable. It's a nice way of releasing physical and emotional tension but *it's not worth all the stress*.' She pushed her palms together then apart and then together again in an endearing gesture of the difficulty she had, revealing such things to him. 'I like my calm life. I like everything the way I have it. I don't need you or any other man, upsetting that and changing things. It's not worth it to me. It's two bodies joining—it's nothing!'

'It's magic,' he protested.

'Nonsense.' Her lovely mouth tightened. 'At best it's pleasant. Because I'm attracted to you I'm sure sex with you would be very pleasant but that's still not enough to make me want it.'

Pleasant? He stared at her, rendered abruptly mute by the insipidness of that word. Yes, he'd had *pleasant* sex in the past. Unemotional, enjoyable, physically satisfying but unextraordinary sex. But that was never how it would be with Maggie.

'Maggie, I look at you and it hurts to breathe,' he said thickly. 'That's not *pleasant*, that's *magic*.'

He saw her swallow and her voice when she spoke was soft and low. 'Will, you're exaggerating a normal part of the body's physiological response to sexual attraction—'

'I'm exaggerating nothing.' He felt torn between despair and exasperation. He didn't know if she was deliberately trying to conceal her feelings or if she really believed what she was saying. 'Humour me,' he said roughly. 'Let me prove to you that there can be magic. Let's experiment.'

'How?' Her suddenly narrowed gaze reflected a cynicism he'd never seen in her before. 'By letting you sleep with me?'

He couldn't resist. 'Would you do that?'

Her face closed. 'No.'

'Then let me just kiss you.'

She slid backwards in her chair and the table jolted a little when it shifted against the leg, but he felt her mental recoil far more strongly.

'Just one kiss, Maggie.' He ached for her. 'If you're so sure it won't be anything special you've nothing to lose.'

'There's no point. One kiss isn't going to make any difference.'

'Prove it to me.'

'But I don't want to.'

'If there isn't any magic I'll leave you in peace.'

He saw her swallow again. Her face was pale but composed and mask-like, and her hands had clenched around the edge of the table so hard that her knuckles had turned white. 'What do you mean?'

'Completely in peace. Friends, colleagues, whatever you want. Nothing else.'

'You are the most astonishingly arrogant man I've ever met,' she said abruptly. 'How in the world can you possibly imagine that I'll let you seduce me with just one kiss?'

He didn't feel arrogant. He felt nervous. 'I'm curious,' he said softly. He was risking a lot on one kiss. He liked that—he liked the challenge. It excited him, but if she didn't respond he was promising her a lot more than he was confident he could deliver.

'All right. One kiss.' She unclenched her hands but promptly put them under the table. 'Why not? It's not as if I've never been kissed before. It won't be so bad. What do you want me to do? Shall I...stand up?'

'Sure.' His mouth quirked at her abruptly defensive stare. 'Relax, Maggie. You said it. It won't be so bad.' He pushed his own chair back quietly and went to her. He drew her stiff, incredible body slowly towards him until he could see the little embers of alarm taking spark in the depths of her eyes—so close that he began to lose himself beneath the sweet spell of her scent. 'You've changed today,' he said softly. 'Something's changed. I can feel it.'

'It's...Christmas,' she whispered. 'It's a special time. Can we get this over with, please?'

'In a second.' He'd never been this close to her before and the sensation was heady. 'You know I fantasise about you, too, Maggie. I fantasise about holding you. About kissing you. About taking away your clothes one small, maddening thing at a time.'

'Will...' Her voice was weak, husky almost, and he brought his mouth closer to capture it. 'Please just do it.'

'I fantasise about making love to you until you can't think of anything but me.' He wanted to make it last longer, he wanted to tease her, but she was soft and exquisite and the total astonishing reality of her in his arms made his head spin. His focus shifting so his concentration was totally on her mouth, he lowered his head.

If he'd asked himself in a more rational moment how he'd deal with a woman determined to resist him, it would never have occurred to him that he would do anything other than desist. But this was Maggie, and it was the first time he'd touched her properly and it felt as if he'd waited a lifetime for her and he didn't desist.

She kept her mouth clamped shut against him, but he used every weapon he had to coax her open, licking her, murmuring against her, easing her lips open until she allowed him access to the wetness he craved.

When she shook her head and tried to twist from him, he took her face between his hands, caressed the silky soft skin of her cheeks and held her so that she couldn't move. But when she still tried, when she went up onto her tiptoes, trying to escape him still, he loosened the clip that held her hair and tugged at it until the long red tresses tumbled around them like a fragrant waterfall of fire. He grabbed at it, twisted it into his fists and wound his hands among its slippery strands so he could grip her and hold her tight.

But still something in her fought him. She kissed him back, let him capture her tongue, drove him to the brink of madness, but their mutual sweet plundering still didn't bring her to complete surrender. Maggie's small palms pushed feebly at his chest, powerless but still unwelcome in that they forced him to recognise that, despite her hunger, she still had some power to resist him.

Will moved, backing her away from the table and against the wall behind them so he could come closer to her and immobilise her fists between the breath-taking pressure of her breasts against his chest.

As if his disabling of her ability to fight him relieved her of the obligation to even attempt it, he felt her finally soften. He felt her surrender herself to the kiss. Without conscious thought he lifted her so that her feet left the ground, supporting her with the weight of his body against her, fitting himself into the contour of her, worshipping her mouth.

She was his. He felt it. He loved it.

But, of course, he couldn't. Not in the impersonal gloom

of the hospital's canteen, no matter how seductive their after-hours isolation. And not when he had work to do— urgent, important work, even if at that moment he'd have traded everything he owned not to have to leave her to go back to that.

Slowly, achingly, he put her from him. His heart was pounding and he closed his eyes briefly, concentrating on controlling himself and on slowing his breathing. His chest ached as if he'd been running. When he opened his eyes he saw that she was breathing just as fast and he allowed himself to feel the satisfaction that gave him even though he saw that she couldn't bring herself to meet his eyes.

'Mrs Adams,' she said thickly.

'I have to go back,' he agreed, his breath still coming fast even though he'd backed a few steps further away from her now. 'You don't have to come with me, Maggie. Finish your dinner. I'll handle this.'

'Yes.' Her voice was subdued, muffled, and the hands that lifted to smooth her gloriously dishevelled hair away from her face and behind her ears were shaking more than they had before he'd touched her. 'I'll come along soon,' she told him.

'Maggie…?' Moving forward again, he took her chin between his thumb and forefinger and lifted it gently, desperate to know. 'Can we hold this space, please?'

'Yes.' There was something terribly appealing and young about the dazed look she finally sent him. 'I suppose. If you want.'

'Of course I bloody want.' His voice half shattered on his wry acknowledgement, and to his joy she smiled, too, a small, dizzying movement but a smile nonetheless. 'Are you all right?'

'I'm not sure.' She was breathless and that pleased him, pleased him utterly.

He brushed his index finger softly across the lower curve

of her mouth. 'You're swollen here now,' he said huskily, his heart starting to throb heavily again. 'Did I hurt you?'

'No.' Her mouth opened just slightly but it was more than enough to bring him back to full and total arousal, and with a muttered curse he spun on his heel. 'I have to go.'

Turning Mrs Adams onto her front and adding nitric oxide had improved things slightly. He spent a few minutes reassuring Mr Adams that at least there'd been no worsening in his wife's condition since he'd changed those things, before scrubbing in preparation for inserting the intravenous line they'd use for filtering her blood.

Maggie was still not back on the unit when Will and Steven finished. He looked around for her automatically although he knew that if she'd returned he would have felt her there. He checked on Mrs Everett, their obstetric patient, spoke briefly with Mr Radcliffe's family, looked over Mr Fale and checked the readings from the Ganz he'd put in earlier, then he went looking for her.

She was still in the canteen. She'd replaced the chair he'd tipped over, as well as her own, at the table, and her hair was up again. She was sitting, but he could see that she hadn't touched her food. She might not have heard him when he'd opened the door because he'd been quiet, but she didn't look around when he let it click closed behind him.

Finally, after a few painful seconds she lifted her head. 'You don't look especially triumphant,' she said quietly, achingly seriously. 'Funny. I've been thinking about it, expecting that you would.'

He took the chair opposite her. Triumphant? The idea was ludicrous. Perhaps, before, he might have considered it a possibility but now, seeing her like this, the idea struck him as impossible. No, what he felt just now was…numb. Dazed, even, as dazed as she'd seemed that first time she'd looked up at him.

'I wish I did feel that way,' he admitted thickly. It was true. Because if he'd been triumphant that would have meant that he could have taken her to his bed now, without in any way damaging his own peace of mind, but instead he wasn't sure that he was going to be able to do that—or if he did do it, he wasn't sure he would be able to live with himself afterwards.

He'd thought these past months that they'd been playing a game. A subtle, adult game which they both understood and one which he'd win if he played it patiently and correctly. Now he saw that he'd been wrong. Maggie had never been playing. Her determination not to become involved had been real. Something had changed. He was no longer sure he wanted to win because the cost could be hurting her.

He liked her, he admired her, he desired her and he wanted her in his bed. But there it ended.

He was comfortable with his life. The things he'd said to Jeremy, about envying him his wife and children, had been sincere but less than complete. It wasn't the wife or the children themselves that he coveted, but rather the contented happiness that Jeremy's family gave his friend. Eventually Will did want his own family but it was a vague ambition and he didn't yet crave such commitment. And when it did happen he pictured a peaceful, gentle, contented, loving woman, someone probably like his mother or perhaps like Jeremy's wife, Catherine, as the mother of his children.

Maggie didn't fit into the image in any way. She was cool and self-contained and defensive and awkward and difficult to read yet underneath, to his disbelief, he understood now that she was also unbearably and achingly vulnerable.

She'd denied being abused in the past but there had to

be something he didn't know. Something had left her wary
of relationships, at least wary of a relationship with him.

With an emotion akin to relief he acknowledged that he
wasn't so self-seeking that he could take advantage of the
weakness he'd finally uncovered. He had nothing to offer
her and suddenly the selfishness of what he wanted from
her appalled him.

'It's quiet on the unit now,' he said gently. 'Prue's putting her truffles out for supper. Come back and have a drink
with us.'

It wasn't to his credit, he conceded, but, predictably, she
looked confused. 'Will—'

'Maggie, leave it. I don't mind.' It was a lie because he
minded terribly and he hated himself for his dishonesty, but
above all he wanted to soothe her. 'It was just a Christmas
kiss. It didn't mean anything. You don't have to worry. I'm
not going to force things any further.'

'A Christmas kiss?'

'I even meant to bring mistletoe from Theatres but I forgot,' he hedged. 'I shouldn't have taken advantage of you.
I'm sorry. I know that wasn't something you wanted. Come
on.' He held out one hand for her. 'If we don't go now
they'll have eaten all the truffles.'

To his mingled pleasure and dismay—pleasure that she
apparently trusted him enough, and dismay at the immediate effect the innocent touch of her hand on the arm he
offered had on his senses—she let him lead her to the doors.

Outside, under the harsh fluorescent lighting of the corridor, she moved away. Wary of doing anything to weaken
his determination to minimise the significance of their embrace, he made no attempt to stop her. 'Prue rang the baby
unit in town,' he said neutrally. 'They're still settling in
Linda Everett's little boy but they're not unhappy with his
condition. They said that his chest X-ray was better than
expected.'

'That's good.'

Her steps were smaller than his and he adjusted his pace to hers. 'Mr Radcliffe's wife and some of his children have been in.' Gradually he could feel things starting to normalise between them and he pressed on, talking of work because at that moment it was all he could trust himself with. 'They bought a pack of Christmas carol tapes for us. The nurses are going to share them around between the patients.'

'Christmas carols? Oh!' She stopped, lowered her head, then looked back at him, her expression profoundly self-conscious. 'I'm sorry but I forgot... That call I took for you earlier. It was your mother. I think some of your family as well. Calling from Auckland. You were busy, talking with George Barnes, so I didn't call you over. They sang to me.'

He winced. 'Sorry. I'd have saved you from that if I'd known what was going on. Was it awful?'

'Pretty much,' she said dully, 'but I quite enjoyed it.'

'That's not easy to believe.' He sent her a sideways look, relieved to see that at least she'd started to smile a little. 'She forces us to go out singing every year around the city. It's a fund-raising thing for some local charities but there's only one or two out of the forty of us who go who can even hold a tune.'

'I guess you don't make a lot of money.'

'Actually, we usually make at least a thousand dollars.'

Her smile lightened suddenly. 'People pay you to go away.'

'Precisely.' He managed what he thought might be a creditable grin.

'Your family sounds very close,' she observed. 'Sad that you couldn't manage to spend Christmas with them this year.'

Sad for whom? he wondered. The realisation that Maggie

wouldn't have missed him if he'd been away was sobering. Now at the unit, they stopped to shed the cotton gowns they both wore over their clothes. 'Maggie, what about your family? Are you missing them?'

'There's only my mother.' Her back was to him as she washed her hands. 'I miss her, of course, but I was home at Easter. I'll call tomorrow morning. That'll still be Christmas Eve in England.'

'No brothers or sisters?'

'None.' She dried her hands and moved back, leaving the basin for him.

He thought about his own family. 'What about aunts, uncles, cousins—that sort of thing?'

'None of the above,' she said flatly, her expression at its most frustratingly cool. 'I'm an only child of only children and my father died almost a decade ago. There's my mother and me, Will. That's it. Why?' Her lovely green eyes flashed a challenge at him. 'Feeling sorry for me?'

'No.' Will considered his family. He wouldn't trade any member for anything and his parents had done their best but it hadn't always been easy, being raised as merely one of a brood of nine. Perhaps Maggie's upbringing accounted for her preference for solitude? 'No, right now, remembering carol nights, the idea of being an only child sounds blissful,' he admitted wryly.

She tilted her head. 'It's obvious you come from a big family. I guessed from the start.'

'How?'

'You have a certain...openness,' she commented obliquely. 'You communicate easily. It was something I noticed immediately about you. I admire that ability. It doesn't come naturally to many people.'

'Maggie, I'm sorry about what happened about the directorship.' She was wrong about his communication skills, at least about his communication skills when it came to communicating with her. When talking with her, he often felt as if he were stumbling about in the dark. But now the words came naturally to him where he'd hesitated in the past, unsure whether it was better simply to let things ride. 'About my taking the job. About you becoming only deputy.'

She'd gone very still. He didn't know what Jeremy had told her and he wouldn't put it past his friend to have failed to mention that he'd had no idea what the true situation had been, but, despite his loyalty to his friend, he wanted to clear the air. He trod gently. 'What I mean is that I'm sorry that you were led to believe that the job would be yours permanently if you came out to New Zealand.'

'You're far more experienced,' she said slowly. 'I was already one of two physicians and there were no full-time anaesthetists on staff. I should have realised earlier. It was common sense to assume they'd be looking for an anaesthetist to take over as director.'

'They were so desperate to get someone with your reputation that they would have said anything to get you out here,' he said gently.

'I don't hold any grudges, Will.' The set of her chin firmed. 'I might have been...disappointed at first but as soon as we started working together I realised that that was short-sighted. You're the best person for the job. From the first day you started there hasn't been any question of that in my mind.'

'And the future...?' He frowned at her questioning look. 'Are you content here? Do you still hold ambitions of going further? Have you made any plans to move on?'

'Not at this stage.' Her face closed again. 'I'm sure you're aware that my visa and contract are only valid for three years at present.'

'If you moved on would you want to stay in New Zealand?' He didn't like himself for the way he was pushing her but still he wanted to know. 'Or would you prefer to go home?'

'I don't know.' She shook her head slightly, as if dismissing that. 'I haven't thought about it.' Leaving him, she pushed open the door into the unit. 'I like it here but if I do leave I shouldn't imagine you'll have any trouble filling my job. It doesn't matter what I do, does it?'

The blare of his anaesthetic bleeper meant he didn't have to answer that, and with a half-sympathetic smile Maggie went around him towards the staffroom while he went into the unit proper to use the telephone. An impersonal voice gave him an extension number to dial. It was the first-on anaesthetic registrar, needing help. 'I've started an appendix case in theatre two but Maternity have called for an epidural,' he told him. 'Sorry about this, Dr Saunders, but do you think you could go?'

'No problem,' Will reassured him, smiling a little at the younger doctor's reluctance to ask him to do something so small. If he'd been a registrar he was fairly sure he'd have enjoyed sending a consultant in his position running about the hospital. 'Nothing else brewing?'

'Nothing surgical in Casualty,' the registrar told him. 'And, apart from this case and one other, Maternity seems quiet so fingers crossed.'

Will looked into ICU's staffroom and grinned. Prue and Maggie and Steven and Tim, as well as a couple of the staff nurses from the night shift, were sipping drinks, and all, apart from Maggie—who seemed intent on the journal she'd retrieved from somewhere—were eyeing a generous foil tray of chocolate truffles. 'Waiting for me?' he teased.

'Of course.' Prue blew him a cheeky kiss. 'Get in here and sit down. You can have sparkling grape or sparkling apple juice.'

'I wish I could but I've been bleeped,' he said wryly.

'Sorry. Maternity calls. Can you hold on another half-hour for the truffles?'

'No,' they chorused cheerfully, diving in.

'None for you,' Prue chimed, her mouth full of chocolate. 'We've been waiting too long already. And don't you turn that smile on me, Will Saunders; I'm a respectable married woman.'

He laughed. 'Maggie, your mission is to save me one,' he ordered. 'Don't let them scoff them all.'

The patient requesting the epidural was a thin young woman in early labour. 'She's only three centimetres and going slowly,' the midwife told him, referring to the amount that the cervix had dilated. Three centimetres suggested early labour—the nearer to ten the further labour had gone. 'She's finding it hard. It's her first and she's very anxious. She's very keen for the epidural and we thought that if we could relax her enough for a few hours then things will go better in the long run.'

Their patient was wearing an automated blood-pressure measuring cuff connected to a monitor, and the midwife had already set up a drip so that they'd be able to give fluids quickly if the epidural led to any drop in blood pressure.

The midwife had also organised a trolley for him and had explained to the patient what he was going to be doing, but he ran briefly over things, before scrubbing his hands and gloving.

Their patient rolled awkwardly onto her side, drawing her knees up as much as possible given the size of her abdomen. 'A little bit cool and wet now,' he warned. 'I'm just cleaning the skin around where the needle will go.'

He worked quickly. Her lumbar vertebrae were easy to feel, and he gently palpated the area he preferred to use between the third and fourth vertebrae. Using a tiny needle, he injected local anaesthetic around the site, gave it a few minutes to work, then introduced the specialised epidural needle into the same area until he felt a familiar 'pop' as it slid into the epidural space.

He aspirated with a syringe as a routine check to make sure that he hadn't accidentally gone through into the spinal fluid, then replaced the needle with a plastic catheter which he filled with two mils of sterile saline and lifted up then down again while he watched the movement of the meniscus of the fluid, a back-up test to check that the line was in the right position. Reassured, he connected the tubing to a small reservoir especially designed for epidural injections, looped the tubing against her skin then taped a sterile dressing over it, leaving the reservoir end loose for the midwife to position however she preferred it.

He checked the contents, dose and expiry date of the Marcain and the pethidine that the midwife passed him, drew up a mixture of the local anaesthetic and opiate and then injected it slowly into the tubing.

'This should last about two hours,' he told their patient, 'sometimes not quite so long. I'm leaving a little plastic tube in your back so we can top it when you need more. The pain relief I've put in here sometimes causes skin itching so if you notice any just let us know and we'll give you something to stop it.'

When they were finished the midwife came back with him to the desk so he could write up the procedure in the notes. 'Thanks, Dr Saunders. I'll keep an eye on the blood pressure. Are you happy for me to top it up when she needs it?'

'Fine.' He signed his note and wrote his bleeper number beside it. 'I've charted Stemetil for nausea and naloxone for itch. Give me a call if there're any problems. I'll come back in a few hours just to check, anyway. Nothing else happening up here?'

'Quiet as anything. How's that wee lass we sent over earlier?'

'As well as we could expect,' he told her. 'She hasn't fitted again.' He told her what he'd told Maggie about the baby. On his way out he paused at the brightly lit Christmas tree in the corner of the foyer. 'What's this?'

'We decided that no one would come snooping around at this stage,' she told him with a smile, correctly interpreting his grin. 'We only put the lights on it after tea, though—we weren't brave enough to do it before that. Even the nursing supervisor helped. We couldn't believe it. She's a grumpy old thing usually and we thought she'd be dead against it. What do you think?'

'That it's fantastic,' he told her easily.

'It's not as if they can sack us,' she said firmly, sounding as if she'd said the same sort of thing several times already. 'Who'd deliver the babies?'

'Exactly.'

The emergency blare of his ICU bleeper started him running even before he'd heard the message. 'Emergency. ICU,' it said. 'Emergency. ICU.'

CHAPTER SIX

MAGGIE was in her office just down the main corridor from the unit, pretending to herself that she was concentrating on the journal she needed to read, when her emergency bleeper went. It only took her a few seconds to get back.

'Bed five,' Tim called urgently as soon as she pushed through the doors.

Steven and Mr Fale's nurse already had the screens around his bed and the defibrillator charged. 'V Fib,' Belinda, his nurse, said breathlessly, referring to the chaotic heart trace displayed on the monitor above their heads. 'We've shocked once at 200 joules.'

'Try the same again,' Maggie instructed, moving one of the electrodes further away from the paddles the nurse held. 'What happened?'

'Clear.' She stood back while Belinda pressed the button on the right paddle and discharged the shock.

'He had two short runs of VT, which is when we bleeped you,' Steven explained. 'Then this.'

They watched the monitor and Maggie let out her breath when, after a few hesitant beats, the rhythm returned to normal. 'Sinus,' she said quietly. 'Well done.'

Tim was sorting the emergency drugs held in the top drawer of the resuscitation trolley. 'Do you want to start a lignocaine infusion?'

'Not yet,' Maggie told him, observing the prominent pulses in Mr Fale's neck and the movement of his heart against his chest wall, both classic signs of overwhelming infection. 'Let's concentrate on getting control of the infection. If he arrests again I'll reconsider. How's his BP?'

'Ninety over seventy,' Tim informed her, moving out of the way so that Maggie could see the monitor. 'Pulse now 110.'

Maggie checked the ventilator readings and the data coming from the Ganz, then made a few swift calculations on the calculator attached to the chart table at the end of the bed. 'How's his urine output?'

'Forty mils this last hour,' Belinda told her, crouching to inspect the bag.

'We have to get more fluid into him.' She opened up the bag of plasma replacement already attached and charted more, then fine-tuned the dosages of the medication infusions. 'He needs all bloods, another three sets of blood cultures, a chest X-ray to look for signs of failure and a twelve-lead ECG.' She moved to examine Mr Fale's abdomen—not easy, given his recent surgery. His wounds looked clean and his colostomy looked reasonably healthy but she couldn't hear any bowel sounds. 'Have Microbiology found any bugs, apart from the ones in the urine?'

'Everything else clear so far,' Steven told her.

Maggie studied their patient worriedly. It bothered her that they were assuming that the only source of infection was the urine, particularly when they were fully treating that and yet he'd still had another episode of shock. 'I'll get the surgeons up to have another look at his tummy,' she said, retreating towards the main station. 'Have we got any relatives in?'

'His son left before tea,' Belinda told her.

'You organise things here and I'll call him,' Tim said, walking with Maggie to the telephones.

Will—summoned, she assumed, by the emergency bleeper—was at Mr Fale's bedside when she finished speaking to the on-call surgeon who, by luck, happened to be the actual consultant looking after Mr Fale. Seeing Will there made every cell in her body want to up and run away but she forced herself to go across.

'Steven explained,' he said, lifting his hand when she started to speak. 'He's thrown off two ectopic beats while I've been here but his rhythm seems otherwise stable. This is his second arrest. Why don't you want to use anything to reduce the risk of another one?'

'The primary problem's his infection,' she told him. 'On echo this afternoon his heart looked strong. Any more trouble and I'll reconsider. The surgeon's coming in to have another look at him. I wouldn't be surprised if he thought there was infection within his abdomen somewhere—it would make more sense.'

'You're worried about a subphrenic?'

'A collection anywhere,' Maggie acknowledged, concentrating on the chart, too self-conscious to look at him directly. A collection of unnoticed infection, possibly subphrenic—under his diaphragm—or elsewhere could account for his failure to respond to antibiotics. 'We've got the radiologist coming in for Mrs Everett. If the surgeon agrees we could ask him to CT Mr Fale at the same time.'

It was difficult to talk to Will like this, more difficult than she'd expected as she'd used work like a barrier between herself and him for the past eleven months now so she'd grown fairly skilled at wielding her professionalism like a shield. 'Have you seen his ECG?' she asked, looking under the day sheet where such things were normally stored. 'Belinda was going to do one.'

'Just about to,' Belinda announced absently, coming towards them. She was wheeling the small machine on a stainless-steel trolley. 'Sorry. We're still struggling through hand-over. You'd think they'd be happy, tucked up in there with their tummies full of Prue's truffles, but they're not. They're starting to yell. Still, it won't do any harm for them to wait a few minutes more.'

'Don't worry, I'll do this.' Maggie took charge of the trolley with a sympathetic smile. Steven was busy organising the blood tests she'd ordered so she was happy to take over the procedure herself. 'You've had a busy night,' she told Belinda. 'It's way past your hand-over time. You must be wanting to get home.'

'I'm only an hour late.' But the nurse's quick smile was relieved. 'Thanks, Dr Miller, that'd be great. I'll run away. It's going to take me half the night to wrap all the kids' presents as it is and I'm on again in the morning.'

'See you then,' Maggie told her. 'Happy Christmas.'

'You, too, Dr Miller. Dr Saunders.' She raced away.

'I'll help.' Will's dark eyes were unreadable as he held out his hand for the ECG stickers.

Taking care not to touch him, Maggie passed him a sheet, then busied herself setting up the machine and sorting the various coloured leads while he stuck the stickers, with their metal domes, in the appropriate places. One went on each leg and arm, one went to the right side of the chest at heart level and the rest went from there in series across the left side of Mr Fale's chest, overlying his heart.

Once the stickers were in place she passed him the leads for the left arm and chest leads while she clipped on the others. The machine was completely automated and once the leads were in place all she had to do was press a single button, detailing the layout of the ECG she wanted. It ran its own test of the system then produced a beautifully printed sheet of the results.

'Sinus tachy,' she told him slowly, reading it systematically and mentioning the fact that, apart from the beat being faster than usual—entirely consistent with widespread infection—the rhythm was normal. 'One ectopic beat on the rhythm strip but I don't think that's worth worrying about now.'

Rather than passing it directly to him—he might see the

shaking of her hands which she was proving completely ineffectual at controlling—she slid the sheet to his side of the bed. 'What do you think?'

'I agree.' His assessment of the recordings was brief. 'I'll leave the stickers on in case we want another one later,' he said, as she automatically began to unclip the leads.

'Good idea.' She spoke mechanically, concentrating only on getting through this. Later she'd work on her wounds—for now her prime objective was just to avoid making a fool of herself again.

'Did you manage to save me a truffle?'

'There're some put away in the fridge.' She'd been too distracted to even remember his order, but Prue, she knew, had made sure there'd been a generous number set aside for him. The staff nurse, like every other nurse on the ward, it seemed, was obviously very fond of Will.

'Did you try them?'

'I wasn't hungry.' Still keeping her eyes averted from his, she folded the leads systematically over the machine, unplugged it and pushed it away. 'His white count at nine was up slightly. Until we get a CT there isn't much else we can do.'

'You should have tried one,' he said quietly. 'I told you they'd change your mind about not having a sweet tooth.'

'I'm really not interested in chocolate.' She folded back the screen guarding the foot of the bed and pushed the machine out. 'Have you heard from the radiologist? Shouldn't he be in by now?'

'He's going to bleep me when he arrives,' he told her quietly. To her dismay he was following her. 'They're not just ordinary chocolate,' he continued, still on, she realised, about Prue's truffles. 'She uses some wonderful stuff imported from Belgium.'

'Really?' she said dully. 'How interesting.'

'They're chocolate covered but inside there's cream and brandy as well. I've never tasted any better.'

'I'm really not interested,' she said stiffly, wondering if he was deliberately provoking her now.

'She only makes them once a year.'

'Then perhaps I'll try one next year.'

'I'll give you mine.'

'I don't want yours,' she said brittlely, sure now that he was trying to rile her. She shoved the trolley into its place beside the resuscitation trolley in the equipment room with less than her customary finesse. Irritation overcoming her embarrassment, she glared up at him. 'Why do you keep talking about them?' she demanded. 'This seems such a silly thing. Why is it so important to you that I eat one of these things?'

'Because...' But then he became silent, and she realised that perhaps for the first time since she'd met him he looked uncertain about something.

'Why? Tell me.' Pressing her rarely held advantage, she found herself unrelenting. 'I don't understand.'

'I don't know,' he admitted finally. 'You're right. It is a silly thing. I just wanted to see your expression when you tasted one. I wanted...' and now his regard darkened '...to watch your face. I wanted to watch you enjoy it.'

An acknowledgement of the symbolism of that dried her mouth.

For a brief moment she let their gazes cling but then she turned away abruptly. She didn't understand him. She didn't understand him and she didn't understand anything that had happened tonight or any of the games he was playing with her.

All these months she'd told herself that she could rise above the sexual stirrings he'd always provoked, but she'd been wrong. The fact that she'd missed him so much this week had shaken her enough to leave her vulnerable to him, and now things were suddenly changing too quickly for her to keep up.

His kiss and her own involuntary but total response to it had shattered her understanding of herself and of what she wanted. She'd put up a token resistance at first, she knew, but she'd fooled neither him nor herself. He'd used the word magic and he'd been right.

Her reaction had astounded her. It had been proof she hadn't ever wanted to have that her marriage had left her unaware of the potential strength of her sexuality. Things had changed. In those minutes after he'd left her she'd finally acknowledged that she wanted to know more. She wanted to know much more. She wanted to know everything.

But when Will had come back he'd acted as if nothing significant had happened, as if nothing had changed, even though for her it felt as if the earth had briefly stopped spinning.

She understood, of course. He was sexually experienced while she, it seemed, despite her marriage, remained a relative novice. It was years since she'd shared her bed, enough in itself to make her nervous, even if her experience prior to that had never been particularly extensive.

But her inexperience had obviously bored him. It was a fact she had to face but she wasn't going to leave herself open to rejection again. She would be cool and careful and utterly professional, and he would never know how deeply that kiss had affected her.

'I'll be in my office if anyone needs me,' she said sharply, heading for the doors, intent now on protecting herself. 'Someone please call me when the surgeon gets here.'

Tim called her back not long afterwards. The surgeon understood why she was concerned about another possible source for Mr Fale's infection and, although he doubted they'd find anything, he agreed that a CT was appropriate, especially as the radiologist was already in the hospital, looking at Mrs Everett.

'We'll go down with him,' he offered, including his registrar who was with him. This meant that, since Steven was there too, Maggie didn't have to go to X-Ray. Unit procedure was that at least two experienced nurses or doctors had to accompany all ventilated patients when they left the unit, and Hine and her successor were still busy with handover.

Will came back about fifteen minutes after they left. He and one of the nurses helped to settle Mrs Everett, then he came to her with the scans. 'No localised haemorrhage and no significant swelling.' He pushed the X-rays up onto the board beside where she sat and they both studied them. 'Her blood pressure's been stable for three hours now,' he said quietly. 'I've spoken to George Barnes. We're going to keep her sedated and ventilated overnight, then start waking her first thing in the morning if all's well.'

Maggie nodded her agreement. 'Any more news on the baby?'

'No change, apparently.'

The phone chimed, interrupting them, and she reached for it automatically. The surgeon looking after Mr Fale was on the other end. 'You were right about the subphrenic,' he told her briskly. 'Fortunately, it looks like we're going to be able to get a decent-sized drain in down here under CT guidance so we shouldn't need to take him back to Theatre. Everything else looks fine. We'll bring him back up when we're finished.'

'They've found a collection and they're draining it,' she told Will, once she'd hung up. 'Hopefully, that'll mean a quick recovery for him. How's Anaesthetics?'

'Quiet.' He lifted one broad shoulder easily. 'There's a

Caesarean booked for early tomorrow but nothing over-night. Everything in Casualty looks minor.'

'Then you should go to bed.' They were alone at the desk now and she lowered her head, studying the drug-company advertising slogan printed along the side of the pen she held. 'It's very late. You must be tired from the flight, and with the two-hour time difference from Sydney you've probably been up hours longer than me. I'll stay around and cover Steven tonight.'

'Firstly, you've got the time difference backwards,' he said smoothly. 'Australia is two hours behind, not ahead. I wasn't at the airport until ten New Zealand time. And I'm not particularly tired. Thirdly, I volunteered for this shift. I'll wait up and check Mr Fale when he comes back.'

'I said I'd ring his son at home to tell him the scan results.'

'I'll call him when I've seen how his father is. Trust me, Maggie. Go to bed.'

'I really don't mind staying up.'

'There's no point because I'll be here. I'll call you if we get swamped.'

'But I feel guilty.'

'Don't be ridiculous. If I were Ian would you feel the same?'

'Ian's a registrar,' she said swiftly. 'It's part of his job—'

'Which means it's part of mine tonight,' he countered.

'That's just you being stubborn,' she said stiffly. She felt terrible about not having thought to ask Ian about his baby herself, especially when she'd noticed that he'd been look-ing tired lately. If she had asked him the reason she'd have told him not to bother coming in today. 'This is a ridiculous thing to argue about.'

'I agree,' he said instantly. 'Go to bed.'

Maggie knew when she was beaten but she moved re-luctantly. 'Have they given you a room?'

'I left it too late to get a key,' he said gruffly. 'I'll sleep on the unit. Stop worrying,' he chided. 'I'll start to think you care.'

'Of course I care.' Doctors who were first on call for the unit were expected to be readily available at all times, but they were permitted to sleep if it was quiet. On a normal night they'd manage two to three hours of broken slumber although there was no general rule. The bed he referred to on the unit was barely an examination couch. It wouldn't be at all comfortable.

On-call staff were supposed to pick up a key to one of the on-call doctors' bedrooms at the top of the block from someone in administration but the keys were available during office hours only.

'You'll never get any sleep on that couch.' She had no choice, she realised. The thought of him being in her home was unsettling but her conscience couldn't leave him to an uncomfortable night, not on Christmas Eve. Speaking briskly to conceal her nervousness, she retrieved her house keys from the pocket of her white coat.

'Take these. I've got spares in my office. It's flat twelve on Hospital Road. It only takes a couple of minutes to get there and the spare bedroom's the first room on the right upstairs. I'll leave the bed made up for you.'

She held her breath but he didn't say anything but a quiet, 'Thank you.' He looked, she thought, almost puzzled. He curled the keys into his fist. 'This is very kind of you.'

'It's Christmas.' She headed for the door. 'Towels and fresh soaps and things are in the cabinet in the bathroom if you want a shower. There's always plenty of hot water. I'll leave a light on outside for you.'

'I'll try not to disturb you.'

'Don't worry, I'm used to it,' she told him, striving for indifference, although her invitation had just guaranteed she'd never get a wink of sleep tonight. Not one. If there really was a jolly fat man with a red outfit and a big sack of toys, she reflected dryly, this would certainly be her night to see him. 'The neighbours are close,' she added by way of explanation, 'and I'm a very light sleeper. I probably won't see you again before morning, Will, so...Merry Christmas.'

'Thanks, Maggie. You, too.'

She felt his gaze prickling at her back all the way down the corridor.

CHAPTER SEVEN

WILL went for coffee once Maggie had gone, lingering over his drink, still bemused. Considering the way he'd behaved tonight, her invitation had been generous. Extremely so, he acknowledged, and even if the idea of lying close to her, albeit in a different room, was guaranteed to give him the sort of physically uncomfortable night he'd not experienced since adolescence, it wasn't an offer he was going to turn down.

Despite his determination now to confine their relationship to a strictly platonic one, he was still curious to see where she lived. His mouth tightened as he recognised the irony of his curiosity being satisfied the night he'd finally given up on getting her into his bed. Not so surprising, though, he thought frustratedly, considering that the whole reason for the invitation was probably that he'd made the loss of his intentions convincing enough to relieve her of any worries in that direction.

He went back to the unit. 'Fairly quiet at the moment.' Tim explained that he was staying on for a double shift. 'Steven's still down with Mr Fale in CT, I'm told, but I don't think we need you for anything just now.'

'I'll have a look around.' The main unit lights had been switched off but each pump and monitor was softly illuminated with dimmed lamps. Will checked each of the beds systematically, talking briefly with the nurses on night duty.

He adjusted Mrs Adams's dopamine infusion and made a few minor changes to her ventilator settings but, as Tim had said, everything else seemed relatively stable. Mr

104

Adams was quietly asleep in a reclining chair beside her bed.

'I'm going to check Theatre,' he told Tim softly. 'I'll be back in an hour or so but bleep me if Mr Fale arrives back in the meantime.'

'Will do.' The other man nodded. 'Did Prue mention that she's left some truffles in the fridge for you?'

Will had forgotten but it was too late to eat them now. 'I'll get them tomorrow.'

Tim looked interested. 'You know, if you're feeling particularly charitable…?'

'I'm not.' Will sent him a sharply amused look. 'Stay away,' he warned. 'Penalty of death.'

'Understood.' The nurse threw an easy salute. 'Just a thought.'

'Forget it,' Will growled. 'If there's just one missing in the morning…'

'I know, I know.' Tim grinned. 'You'll know who to blame,' he said cheerfully.

'Let me know if Mrs Adams's alarm goes off again.'

He'd been too busy earlier to make it to Theatre's Christmas Eve celebrations but he looked in now, wincing at the noise which greeted him when the automatic doors slid open. While they might be quiet tonight, workwise, sound-wise that wasn't the case, and the volume of the carols, blaring from the portable stereo now adorning the bauble-covered reception desk, almost knocked his head off. 'Have I missed the party?' he shouted.

Amidst a cheerful chorus of Christmas greetings from the nurses who were busy decorating the foyer, Ngaire, the senior nurse on for the night shift, directed him to the kitchen.

'There's still some punch left on the bench,' she shrieked. 'Then come back.' Her feet were bare and she was up on tiptoe on top of a chair, fully stretched and struggling, trying to fasten a silver star to one of the green direction signs which hung just beneath the ceiling. 'We need your height.'

'I'll do it now.' With his hands at her waist, he swung her down, acknowledging the mock-flirtatious way she fluttered her eyelashes at him with an easy smile. He'd known Ngaire since his first year in Wellington as an anaesthetics registrar and she was happily married to one of his colleagues and the mother of two young boys.

Much taller than her, he held the star effortlessly to the sign. 'All right?'

'A centimetre to the left,' she instructed, with her hands on her hips, glaring at him when he rolled his eyes. 'Straighter. Not so high. That's...fine.'

He twisted the support wire into place. 'Anything else?'

'We want different things all along,' one of the other nurses shouted cheerfully. 'Every sign.'

'Pass them up.' Resigned to being kept busy for at least a little while, he moved the chair to the next sign, taking the angel someone passed him. A few minutes later, somewhat bemusedly, he found himself humming along to the music.

By the time they'd finished the whole of the hospital side of Theatres was ablaze with colour. They'd hung tinsel and bells and balloons and decorations from one end to the other, and virtually every surface left uncovered had been stencilled with seasonal greetings in either fake snow or glitter.

'Thanks, Will.' Ngaire stood back, eyeing their efforts with delight. 'What do you think?'

'Surreal,' he said, laughingly dodging a plastic stem of mistletoe a couple of the younger nurses had been teasing him with and which now had been left suspended across the antlers of a laughing plastic reindeer above his head.

'But I like it. We never went to this much trouble in Wellington, did we?'

'In Wellington they never tried to tell us we weren't allowed to,' she said cheerfully.

'Ah.' He eyed her sideways, understanding. 'So this is anarchy.'

She sent him a quick smile. 'We like to think of it as the Christmas spirit reasserting itself.'

One of the telephones had rung a few seconds earlier and now the person who'd answered it called out. 'Ngaire, Maternity's on the phone.' Someone immediately turned down the music. 'They need to bring forward that Caesarean they'd booked for the morning. Are we ready?'

'They can start straight away,' Ngaire agreed immediately. 'Theatre three's already set up and I turned the heating up earlier just in case. Cathy, just check it for me now, please. The incubator should be on already. You and Liz, scrub,' she added briskly, looking around at the other staff. 'Tama, check with Paediatrics that they know what's happening, then go help Liz. I'll call Special Care and make sure someone's told them.'

Going to the phone on the wall nearest them, she dialled a number. In an aside, she said, 'Will, is this Mrs Clary one of yours?'

'I don't know her.' If Mrs Clary was the case the first-on anaesthetics registrar had mentioned earlier, the woman originally booked for the morning, then the registrar was handling it himself. Deciding to stick around in case the younger doctor needed a hand, he carried the chair he'd been using for the decorations back behind the desk so that there'd be room for the bed to come through, then went to make sure things were set up properly in theatre three's anaesthetic room.

Mrs Clary arrived a few minutes later, her serene calm belying the speed with which Will had seen her obstetrician racing towards the changing suite. 'The Christmas decorations,' their patient said dreamily. 'I've never seen so many. They're beautiful.'

'Why, thank you.' Ngaire, who'd come with her from Reception, was working fast at checking Mrs Clary's details both on her wristband and verbally, but she was obviously delighted that her patient had noticed, and her dark eyes sparkled at Will from above her mask. 'You've made it all worthwhile.'

'Epidural in place and working beautifully,' Peter Lee, the anaesthetics registrar, told Will in an undertone. 'This'll be fine. I can manage. Where's our dad?'

'Here he comes.' Ngaire opened the door smoothly to let in a flushed man who was wearing his theatre top backwards. 'In this way, Mr Clary. That's right.' She guided his hands to one of his wife's and then at Peter's nod she opened the doors leading directly through into the operating room. 'Let's go.'

Will helped to push the trolley through, intending to leave them, but he saw that Peter suddenly looked concerned.

'Have we got a paediatrician?' He was looking around quickly, obviously preoccupied as he put up the rail which would separate the surgeon's field from his own. Within seconds the obstetrician and scrub nurse had sterile guards clipped around the rail, and the surgeon's urgency was obviously worrying him. 'Where's the paediatrician?'

'He knows he's needed,' Ngaire said. 'He was busy in Special Care but he'll be here.'

'Better bleep him again in a few minutes if he hasn't come.' Peter didn't look reassured. He turned to Will. 'Dr Saunders…?'

Will tied a mask around his face. 'I'll stay,' he said quietly. In an emergency Caesarean the anaesthetist potentially had two patients as either the mother or the baby could need resuscitation. Traditionally, to minimise the risk to the baby, paediatric staff were present at the delivery. Remembering his own days as a junior doctor, Will empathised with Peter's anxiety about being left alone with both responsibilities.

'Thanks.' The younger anaesthetist looked relieved. 'OK, go ahead,' he told the surgeon.

Ngaire had organised a chair for Mr Clary beside his wife and she alternated between tiptoes and crouching, chatting cheerfully about nothing much at all once Mr Clary had told her that he didn't feel strong enough to look at what was happening.

'It's very hot,' he said weakly, and, glancing at him, Will could see his forehead sweating above his mask.

'The heating's turned up in here to make it better for the baby,' Ngaire explained. 'You'll be fine. Take some deep breaths. It won't be long now.'

Will scrubbed his hands then busied himself at the trolley beside the warmed incubator the nurses had prepared, making sure that he had everything he might need. When the paediatric registrar still hadn't arrived by the time the surgeon was beginning his first fine muscle cuts into the uterus he scrubbed again.

'Meconium-stained fluid,' the surgeon announced quietly. 'I'll need suction as I deliver the head.'

Will pulled on gloves. The staining of the amniotic fluid that surrounded the baby suggested that the baby had been under stress and could be a warning of problems ahead with the infant's breathing.

One of the theatre nurses who'd scrubbed earlier had been standing to one side, her job being to collect the baby. Seconds later she bought her to him, a small, wrinkled, wriggling baby girl.

'Dr Saunders just needs to check her first,' the surgeon

told Mrs Clary cheerfully. 'Then we'll give her back to you. She looks terrific.'

Will agreed. Because of the surgeon's comments about the amniotic fluid he gently suctioned the baby's nose and mouth while the nurse helped him by holding an oxygen mask above her tiny face. But her airways were clear, and the noise or probing obviously irritated the infant because she let out a vigorous and very indignant cry.

'She's fine.' Automatically assessing her colour and movements, Will stood back so that the nurse could take the baby back to her parents. 'Congratulations.'

He almost ran into the paediatric registrar on his way out as the younger doctor came hurtling in. 'Baby's fine,' he said reassuringly.

'Thank God,' the registrar said breathlessly. 'I got stuck in Special Care. I didn't think they were going to be so quick here. So, no problems?'

'Meconium in the amniotic fluid but Apgar nine at one minute,' he told him. 'Merry Christmas.'

'Thanks. You, too.' The registrar continued into theatres while Will went to the changing room.

He shed his mask and the paper hat he'd been wearing then took a brief shower, before changing into fresh blues.

Mr Fale was back on the unit. His new drainage bag contained almost half a litre of murky fluid, and his heart rate and the amount of oxygen he was requiring had both reduced, suggesting a good response to the drainage of the infection.

Will called Mr Fale's son to give him the good news, then checked with Tim and Steven that there was nothing else worrying either of them before he headed across to Maggie's flat. He took the longer route outdoors rather than through the hospital's enclosed corridors, appreciating the chance to clear his head. The slight breeze which had been blowing earlier had freshened a little, but it was still warm and clear and the stars were bright.

As she'd promised, Maggie had left on an outside light and he easily picked out her flat from a collection of about twenty very similar ones. Built on site the year before to provide staff accommodation, the units were modern and town-house style. While he acknowledged that they were certainly a step up from the generally appalling grade of staff housing provided by hospitals he'd worked at in the past, he was still surprised she'd stayed so long in one.

Properties in the district around the hospital and even in some of the more picturesque sites directly overlooking the coast weren't particularly expensive when compared with city prices, and it wouldn't have cost her too much to have bought somewhere less regimented with a good view. Certainly, if she'd sold her home in London, before coming out, she could have afforded to buy a mansion here. And prices were rising now. It struck him as a sensible idea to buy locally quickly.

But then he drew himself up sharply, frowning. The truth was that he had no idea if Maggie had sold her London home, or even if she'd ever owned one. And he had no business wondering about it. Nor, he acknowledged grimly, had he any right to make any assumptions about what she should or shouldn't be doing financially.

Who was he to talk about behaving sensibly? He harboured too much of a sentimental attachment to the aged house he'd bought fifteen years earlier to sell that and move, even though living in Wellington often meant two hours' commuting time every day.

Besides, she might have made a deliberate decision not to buy, he acknowledged grimly. Despite her comments today about having made no plans to move on, she could, in fact, not want to establish herself too strongly for the very reason that she had every intention of moving away the minute she got a better offer.

Will didn't want to go into why he didn't want to think about that.

Assuming Maggie would be long asleep, he took care to let himself in quietly, but once inside he saw that there were lights on downstairs and he could hear the muffled sound of her voice coming from the other end of the flat. He tensed. He'd always assumed she lived alone but she'd never confirmed that. It was entirely possible, he realised belatedly, that he'd been wrong.

He allowed the door to click shut audibly behind him in the hope that she'd realise he'd arrived, and went towards the light.

'OK, Mum. You, too.' Before he reached the room at the end of the hall her words indicated that she was on the telephone, not speaking to someone in person. It sounded as if she was ending her conversation. 'Me, too,' she said. 'OK. Have a lovely day. Merry Christmas. Bye. Bye.'

'Your mother?' He leaned against the doorframe and spoke quietly, not wanting to startle her but at the same time wanting to distract himself from the alluring picture she made. Her lovely hair loose and tangled about her shoulders, her eyes wide, her long legs bare, and wearing only, as far as he could tell, a worn, over-sized T-shirt, she looked young and bemused and utterly desirable. 'From England?' he added thickly, his hands curling unconsciously into fists by his side. 'It's the middle of the night.'

'She's never been very good at working out the time difference,' Maggie said huskily. 'I've explained it to her dozens of times but it doesn't seem to sink in. For some reason now she seemed to think we were twenty-three hours ahead instead of just the thirteen. You'd think it would be easy to remember, eleven hours in their summer and thirteen in their winter, but she never gets it right.'

He saw that she looked confused. 'Is something wrong?'

'No. No, I don't think so.' She blinked up at him. 'Sorry, I'm babbling, aren't I?' She seemed to take a deep breath. 'No, on the contrary, she sounds very happy. It's just that something just occurred to me when I was talking to her. There was a note in her voice when she was talking about…well, I think I've been very naïve.'

'Naïve?' Frowning, he took a few steps towards her, his concern for her overcoming any worries about his possible reaction to being close to her. 'About what?'

'My mother and Patrick.' She looked vague. 'It seems so strange that I never realised before. He was there, of course, well, he's almost always there when she calls, and he said hello, he always says hello, he's a very nice man, but I just suddenly realised…'

'Who's Patrick?' he probed, when she still looked confused.

'My mother's partner. She's a GP,' she explained hastily when he frowned. 'My father and Mum and Patrick were in practice together for years. Patrick's wife used to nurse with them. After Dad died they took on another younger man, and a few years later Patrick's wife died. She was quite young. It was ovarian cancer…about seven or eight years ago now.'

'And your mother and Patrick…?'

'I think they're together.' She looked at him. 'I mean together, together. They've always been good friends and he's been around a lot the last few years. I suppose knowing that she wouldn't be alone was part of the reason I felt so happy about coming out here. But I just realised that they're more than just friends. Patrick's son's been working in South Africa for a few years and Patrick's just been down there for two weeks, visiting him. Mum was saying how happy she was that he was back now. She said she'd missed him terribly even in just those two weeks…'

She looked away from him then but he saw her blink several times. 'She's only fifty-seven,' she continued quietly. 'I forget, most of the time, how very young she is. Of course I should have realised that she'd want someone. I just can't believe I never guessed.'

'But when you were at home this year…?'

'Well, he was at the house quite a lot and I remember he stayed over once after one of Mum's dinner parties…but he'd had a few glasses of wine with his meal and I just assumed he was staying in one of the spare rooms. It never occurred to me that there was anything more to it than that.'

'Your mother's never said anything?'

'Perhaps she thought I'd disapprove.'

'Would you?'

'Of course not.' But she looked unsure. 'I mean…it's been ten years. She deserves to be happy. I like Patrick. And it's her life, not mine.'

'Perhaps you should let her know how you feel.'

'I will.' She nodded, but he saw that she still looked a little lost. 'I will,' she repeated. 'You know, she was always so happy with Dad. I think in the past I might have found it difficult to understand why she'd want anyone else. I don't mean as a friend, of course, anyone would understand that. I just mean as—'

'A lover,' he supplied softly.

'Yes.' She sent him a quick, almost shy look. 'A friend becoming a lover seems like a very complicated change to go through. I think I might have wondered why she wanted to bother.'

'You're speaking as if your thinking has changed on that.'

'I suppose it has.' She was knotting her fingers together. 'Now. In some ways. You must think I sound very stupid.'

'Never stupid.' Nervous, innocent and shy, he realised, fascinated by her. 'Inexperienced, perhaps.'

'That's one way of putting it.' She uncoiled her legs, her bare feet swinging to the ground. 'And you don't have to tell me that I'm sounding pathetic because I know it already.'

'Not pathetic,' he said quietly, but she wasn't listening to him. She'd already gone to the kitchen.

'It's very late,' she called. 'Would you like a coffee or a soft drink or are you too tired?'

'Something cold sounds good.' The breeze, stirring the curtains, meant the air inside the flat was the same temperature as the night outside, but he had to counter the provocative effect Maggie had on his body's own internal temperature control.

Idly he lifted one of the cassette tapes she'd left on the coffee-table, grimacing as he saw that it, along with its companions, was a recording of a recent symposium on cardiac emergency care he knew she'd attended.

'This is nice,' he commented, looking around. He didn't mean the decor or the furnishings, of course, which, as far as he could see, were largely standard, cheap and nasty and hospital-supplied, but there were touches of her.

Touches which pleased him, he realised, going to inspect the vivid Matisse print which dominated one wall. It was a work he'd always liked and he was a little surprised that their tastes matched so closely.

She'd put a huge ceramic vase below the print. Bold and colourful, it was filled with red and cream lilies. Christmas lilies, they were called in New Zealand, for that was when the blooms were at their visual and fragrant best, and now their strong, spicy scent filled the room and he inhaled it appreciatively.

He questioned her about the print when she returned with what looked like a lemonade for each of them.

'The Matisse?' she said. 'Yes, it's one of my favourites. I had to have something to brighten the place up.' She grimaced generally at the furniture. 'I brought hardly anything out from England. When they offered me a furnished place I realised it wasn't worth the bother. Graham wanted most of the furniture when we separated and the few things I still had I simply put into storage.'

'Graham?' He took a deliberately slow mouthful of his lemonade, hoping she'd add something, but when she didn't he said, 'Your husband?'

'We're divorced.'

'Did you split up quite soon before you came out here?'

'No, actually, quite a long time before.' She looked down into her drink, the curve of her neck where he could see it through the curtain of her hair achingly vulnerable. 'But in the years up until I came out here I'd been working long hours and practically living in at the hospital. He took the house, you see.' She spoke very softly. 'It seemed like the most sensible thing since, well, since…' He saw her swallow and thought she was going to stop, but she didn't. 'His girlfriend was having a baby,' she continued. 'She's had two now. A boy and a girl. They seem very happy.'

'He had a girlfriend?' He didn't even try to hide his incredulity. This…Graham had had Maggie yet he'd taken a mistress? To him, right now, seeing her like this, such behaviour seemed utterly incomprehensible.

'It was very complicated.'

'It sounds pretty bloody straightforward to me,' he said harshly. 'The man's a lunatic.'

'He was just trying to do the right thing.'

'Like hell,' he countered, still incredulous. She'd been betrayed, which explained at least her reluctance to trust him and the vulnerability he'd glimpsed earlier, but her defence of her ex-husband now left him bewildered.

'We'd already drifted a long way apart,' she said quietly, finishing her drink. 'I don't think there's anything to be gained by discussing this,' she added—unnecessarily because her body language had already told him that she felt that and more. 'It all happened a long time ago and I have no idea why I even brought it up. Would you like another L and P?'

'No. It's probably just thinking about your mother's relationship that's made you remember your marriage.' He emptied his glass then pushed it aside. He willed her to look at him, catching her arm and then her hand when she stood, obviously about to leave him. 'Don't, Maggie. Stay. Talk to me.'

'It's late.' She tugged at her hand but it was like a link with her and he didn't want to let it go.

'Ten minutes.' When her arm loosened and he felt her resolve falter he realised that her mother's call must have shaken her more than she'd admitted. Another chink, he thought, hating himself.

Telling himself that all he wanted to offer was comfort, he tugged her down to him and held her within the shelter of his arms. Her back was stiff against his chest but he nuzzled her hair, half believing his own pretence that that was all he was going to do but still unable to stop himself inhaling her scent shamelessly. 'Not yet. Don't go yet,' he murmured. 'Sit with me.'

'I don't think this is a very good idea,' she said weakly.

He knew it wasn't, but it felt so good that he wasn't going to let her move. 'You smell nice.'

'It's just shampoo. I washed my hair this morning.'

'I like it.' He stroked it gently, lifted some soft strands and let them brush his face.

She was letting him hold her but that was all. She was still very stiff so he folded one arm across beneath her neck to her other shoulder and coaxed her back against him. 'Relax,' he soothed, his mouth at her forehead. 'This is comfortable, isn't it?'

'Yes.' But she sounded unsure and she hadn't relaxed,

not fully. He could feel it in the muscles that strained against him. 'What about the unit?' she asked him, the breathy catch in her voice pleasing him although he hated himself for that pleasure. 'Do you think one of us should call and see if they need anything?'

'I've just been.' Quietly he explained about Mr Fale and everyone else and about how he'd been held up in Theatres.

'A Christmas baby,' she whispered, when he told her about the delivery. 'How lovely.'

'Not for the poor baby,' he said feelingly. 'She'll never get her proper share of presents.'

'You sound like you're speaking from experience.'

'I am.' He grimaced. 'My birthday's two days away. Half the time when I was a kid even Mum would forget.'

'Oh, poor Will,' she said lightly. 'How sad.'

But he'd felt the chuckle she'd suppressed and he tightened his grip around her. His right hand held her now just below the lifting curve of her left breast and, knowing that that was the surest way he could possibly guarantee she'd wrench herself away, it was taking every ounce of self-control he possessed to prevent it from sliding up to cup her. 'Horrible woman,' he growled, breathing deeply. 'Now I've told you my birthday you've got no excuse. I expect a present.'

'I'll buy you chocolate,' she told him, her soft laugh and the relaxation of her back against him igniting a fire inside him. 'Now I know your one weakness.'

'You might be surprised,' he said rawly, aching for her. 'I have other weaknesses.'

'Bikinis,' she said confidently.

Will groaned. 'Forget everything Jeremy has ever told you,' he instructed, still keeping his hand unmoving but unable to stop himself from touching his mouth very lightly to the smooth, soft skin of her forehead. Gently, so gently he was sure she couldn't tell, he let his tongue brush against her. 'The man's not to be trusted.'

'And you are?'

The question was sceptical but the way her beautiful lashes fluttered down as he let his mouth slide a fraction lower was sensuously trusting.

'Not one inch,' he conceded, his breath against her skin, tempted beyond bearing. 'Open your mouth.'

'I thought you weren't going to kiss me ever again?'

'I've changed my mind.' His voice was gravelly but he couldn't help it. He'd barely touched her but the feel of her, pliant like this in his arms, was more erotic than any other woman had been to him naked.

Unable to stop himself, he let his hand cup her, her sharp intake of breath as exquisitely tormenting as the delicate firmness of her breast against his trembling palm.

He caressed her softly. 'Open your mouth, Maggie.' He wanted her desperately but there was no hurry. He felt as if they had all the time in the world. Last time he'd set out to seduce her. Now, he realised, he wanted her to offer her lovely mouth to him herself. 'Let me taste you,' he whispered. 'Let me make love to you.'

CHAPTER EIGHT

LET him make love to her? At that moment, with Will's voice raw and insistent against her ear and his hand working unbelievable magic at her breast, Maggie couldn't think of anything she wanted more. But she remembered what had happened earlier in the canteen and that was enough to make her resist now.

'I thought you didn't want me,' she protested.

'No.' It was a groan. 'I've always wanted you.'

'You said it was a Christmas kiss.'

'Because it's Christmas.' He had been caressing her breast through the cotton of her T-shirt but now his other hand came up and lifted the fabric, scrunching it above her panties. His fingers splayed at her hip, sending shards of heat shivering across her skin. 'God, Maggie.' He was breathing very fast and his urgency now where he'd been so controlled sent her senses spinning. 'You're driving me mad. Give me your mouth.'

But she'd done that earlier and he'd rejected her, and now it wasn't easy for her to trust him. She didn't want to leave him—the way he was touching her felt too good for that—but she needed reassurance.

She moved, swivelled, came around onto her knees on the couch to face him. 'Will...?'

'Don't look at me like that.' He came after her so that she fell from the couch only he caught her and cradled her in his arms as he rolled after her, his mouth warm at her throat as he tumbled over her onto the floor. 'Not scared. I don't want to hurt you, Maggie. I just want to make love to you.'

'I thought you wanted that before?' Underneath him now, her hands in the thick softness of his hair, she held him, needing him to talk to her regardless of the disturbing pressure of his thighs between her legs. 'But then you stopped.'

'I promise not to stop,' he groaned.

But it wasn't enough. 'I don't understand,' she said.

'I sensed you'd been hurt,' he told her finally. 'Your husband, perhaps…a stranger, I didn't know. I thought you were too…vulnerable.'

Maggie froze. She felt herself growing cold. 'And now…?' she demanded, abruptly sober despite the intoxicating touch of him. 'What do you think now?'

He'd felt her resistance, she could tell, and slowly he stilled above her. His hand released her breast, slid lower to her midriff below her shirt then stopped. Slowly, when she did nothing, he rolled away. 'Maggie…?'

'Let me guess.' She felt sick. Wrenching her T-shirt down so that it covered her to her thighs she rolled away and got up onto her knees, her arms crossed protectively across breasts which still ached from his touch. 'Let me guess,' she repeated. 'Now you think, poor Maggie, rejected by her husband for another woman. I know how to make her feel better.'

'No!'

She saw his instinctive move towards her and jumped to her feet and quickly moved back. Still shielding herself with one arm, she held the other outstretched towards him defensively. Everything, everything that had happened just now suddenly made perfect sense to her.

'You've spent your career making people better, Will. You know when to stop but still it bothers you when you know there's nothing you can do for them.'

'Maggie, wait!' He looked genuinely distraught but she didn't believe that he could be. 'Listen to me.'

'I don't want to.' She'd been wrong to think that she'd bored him tonight. He still wanted her. The reason he'd pulled back earlier was because he'd sensed how much his embrace had meant to her. She'd panicked him. She'd been too intense. 'I don't need you,' she whispered. She was furious and she felt humiliated. 'Don't you dare feel sorry for me.'

'I don't,' he responded, and his quietness was enough to calm her a little. He'd sagged back on to his heels, half crouching, and now he regarded her with a brooding watchfulness that she found no less disturbing than his earlier arousal. 'I don't feel sorry for you. Maggie, I understand why you're thinking that now but you're wrong.'

'It makes perfect sense.'

'It makes a crazy, warped sort of odd sense,' he acknowledged, 'but you're still wrong. The problem is that now I haven't a clue what I'm supposed to do.'

'You're not *supposed* to do anything,' she whispered. 'The fact that you're trying to do what you think you're supposed to do is the reason we're in this mess. Do what you want to do.'

He took a heavy breath. 'If I'd done what I wanted to do in the first place then both of us would have been discovered hours later naked and exhausted on the canteen floor.'

Involuntarily her mouth twitched at the image. She sagged. 'Oh, bloody...hell,' she said weakly. 'Really?'

'Really.'

She didn't know whether to laugh or cry. 'What are we going to do?'

'I don't know, Maggie Miller.' He saw the humour, too, she realised, because his mouth relaxed. He came to her and tugged her upright and hugged her and he was suddenly warm again and human. 'I really don't know. I've never heard you swear before.'

'I don't think I ever have,' she admitted, her voice muffled against the soft cloth of his blues. He was big and he was warm and, despite the leap in her senses that being close to him provoked, at that moment he was utterly comforting. 'This is ridiculous.'

'Yes.'

'If you felt like that why did you change your mind?'

'I realised how selfishly I was behaving.' The words rumbled through his chest at her. 'I have nothing to offer you.'

'I didn't ask for anything.'

'You don't strike me as the sort of person who drifts carelessly from affair to affair.'

'I'm not,' she conceded. She pushed back with her palms and looked up at him. It wouldn't be easy, working so closely together, but their affair would probably be very brief and it wouldn't be conducted in public. Now, tonight, close to him like this, seeing that he was as confused as she was, she decided that she could trust him.

'I don't have any particular moral hang-ups about sex,' she said slowly. 'At least I don't think so, not more than most other people.'

Daringly she lifted one small hand to trace the roughened line of his lower jaw. 'I've just never thought I'd ever be interested enough in the act itself to bother with it again. Not until now,' she added, gently emphasising those final words so that there would be no more misunderstandings.

Even with the lamp shining from behind him she could tell that he was frowning. 'Are you telling me that you're not looking for anything permanent?'

'I've had a husband,' she said huskily. 'Marriage is not an experience I have any desire to repeat.'

'Surely, in the beginning—'

'We were young and very inexperienced,' she countered lightly, although, of course, none of the emotions she'd felt at the end had seemed light at the time. She'd dated Graham throughout their time at medical school. Shy and even quieter than she, she'd been the only girl he'd ever been out with. She'd been far more romantic then than she was now and at the time none of that had seemed to matter.

They'd been young, in love, she'd thought, although later, looking back, she'd decided it had been a very immature, mutually dependent sort of love, and in their final year of study they'd married.

Her parents had been hesitant, of course, as had his, at first. They were all doctors themselves and, as such, must have been acutely aware of the pressures those first harrowing working years after graduation could have on relationships and of how very fast they'd be forced to grow up and mature, but they hadn't intervened.

She and Graham had obtained house jobs at the same hospital, and from the blissful perspective of life as students it had seemed as if they'd be able to spend a lot of time together. Of course, it hadn't worked out that way. Both on busy jobs, where the on-duty weekly hours often exceeded a hundred before the extra time needed for study was even counted, they'd barely seen each other for the first six months and the next six had been little better.

Nothing had slowed after that. Despite him arguing that they'd be better off if she went into general practice, Maggie had been determined to continue in hospital training, and for the first time with him she'd refused to give in. Work, despite its demands, had fascinated and fulfilled her. Like him, she'd trained to be a specialist physician, a long process with countless hours on call, including two years where they'd worked in different hospitals in different parts of London and had seen each other sometimes only once a week.

They'd stayed married but the process, together with her total absorption in her work, had changed both of them irreversibly. Whenever she had a chance to draw breath or time to consider things it seemed that years had passed and they had nothing in common any more. Graham was no longer shy and needing her support, and she no longer gave it thoughtlessly.

But they were friends and it seemed there was nothing to be gained by changing anything. As Graham's family was very religious and vehemently opposed to divorce it seemed easier to allow things to continue.

'What went wrong?' Will said quietly. 'Aside from the other woman. Am I allowed to ask?'

'A lot of years when we hardly saw each other,' she replied. 'Then I thought we were going to try and make things work again and I made a sacrifice I should never have agreed to.'

'A sacrifice?'

'We both had cardiology jobs at the same hospital. I'd known for a while that what I really wanted to do was intensive care but I didn't realise Graham was thinking about that, too. A job came up. There were a number of applicants but he was sure that we were the favourites. I let him talk me into dropping out.'

'To continue cardiology?'

'To have a baby,' she said huskily.

He frowned. 'You were pregnant?'

She shook her head. 'Graham kept talking about not wanting us to leave a baby too late and I realised that I was starting to feel that I wanted one, too. I thought it would be good for both of us and for our marriage. At that stage I resigned myself to having to put work on hold for six months after the birth and so, since that would be difficult in the ICU job, I withdrew my application.'

'And he got the job?'

'Actually, no.' There it got complicated. 'He wasn't one of the favourites—he'd been wrong. I was, but when I turned it down it went to someone else. Six months later I reapplied and got accepted into the programme immediately.'

'What about the baby you wanted?'

'It didn't happen,' she said softly. 'Rebecca—his girl-friend—was already pregnant. Graham knew, apparently, or so she told me, although he denied it half-heartedly. She was a nurse on the coronary care ward where we both worked. It was a clichéd case of the wife being the last to know.' She grimaced at the memory.

'It had been going on a long time. I'd had no idea. She told me that he'd promised her he'd marry her but unfortunately by then he'd still not managed to get around to telling me.'

'He didn't want to say anything until he'd persuaded you to drop out of competition for the job,' he said quietly.

'I suspect it was something like that,' she admitted.

'So you lost your job and your husband at the same time?'

'I was annoyed about the job,' she reflected grimly.

He laughed. 'You single-minded career-women are all the same,' he teased. 'Heartless.'

'I'm not really.' She lowered her eyes. Despite the relative ease of telling Will, nothing had been as straight-forward or as painless as she'd made it sound. 'It took me a long time to get over it.'

'Are you?' he asked deeply.

'Mostly, I think.' She still had little feathery doubts about the wisdom of what she was letting herself in for but they weren't enough to stop her now, not when she'd had such a devastating taste of what he could do to her. She lifted a shaky finger and trailed it along the enticing skin around the edge of the V of his shirt's neck. 'So, if the offer's still open, I would like to have sex, please.'

'The offer's still open.' He lowered his face into her

neck, his mouth warm and seeking, and the hands at her hips slid lower to cup her buttocks and lift her provocatively against him.

'It's four in the morning,' she whispered, smiling when he bit playfully at the finger she lifted to the hard curve of his mouth. 'Have you got the energy?'

'The energy,' he confirmed gruffly. 'Always for you I'll have the energy, but I suspect now is not the time.' Instead of looking at his own watch, he took her wrist and checked hers. 'It really is four. I have to get back.'

She loved the reluctance she could feel in him as he squeezed her against him briefly, before releasing her. 'Theatre?'

'ICU. I told Tim I'd be back by three and that's long gone.'

'I'll come with you.' She stepped back and smoothed down her T-shirt. 'Give me a few seconds to get dressed. I'd like to check on Mrs Adams.'

'Maggie, I'll look at her,' he said, coming to the bottom of the stairs when she started up them. 'Don't worry. Go back to sleep.'

But one thing she very definitely could not have done at that moment was sleep and she could tell from his wry smile that he easily interpreted the shy look she sent him. 'Thirty seconds,' she promised. He was still in his theatre blues but there was no way she could go to the hospital in what she was wearing.

She quickly pulled on sports pants and a matching pullover, then slid her feet into slip-on sandals and twisted her hair up, fastening it with a broad clip on top of her head. She hurried back down to him. Her bleeper and white coat were downstairs where she'd taken them off on arriving home and she collected them on her way out.

If Will approved of her more disciplined appearance his neutral expression when he met her nervous gaze didn't reveal it, and she berated herself for being so sensitive to his opinion. 'How was Linda Everett doing when you left?' she asked crisply, closing the door behind them.

'Her blood pressure's stayed down,' he told her. To her surprise, he caught one of her hands and clasped it within his, his strides not faltering. 'Mr Radcliffe was a little more awake. By morning we should have his sedation almost down.'

Maggie was still struggling to come to terms with the way he was holding her hand. She liked it, unquestionably she liked it, but that didn't mean she was comfortable with it. It had been years since anyone had touched her with such...casual intimacy and she'd forgotten how she was supposed to react.

It seemed like such a ludicrously trivial thing to worry about, only just then she could think of nothing else. Her hand felt stiff and awkward—she was merely letting him hold it—but should she be holding him, too? She realised she'd like to—she'd like to be able to let her thumb move softly across his palm the way his thumb was caressing her now—but it seemed an incredibly intimate movement and she didn't know if she had a right to do something like that.

He was still talking. He'd said something about the Christmas decorations in Theatre, and now he was pointing out the huge, brightly lit tree and the Christmas lights blinking out from behind the windows of Rutherford, one of the elderly care wards, but, apart from automatically looking where he'd told her, she was concentrating only on the meeting of their hands.

Finally, gathering courage as they were now almost at the side entrance door she always used to get in after hours—guarded by a monitored security camera, the lock on the door required a keyed code to open—she curled her fingers around his hand and held him as he held her.

She'd held her breath but his reaction was gratifyingly immediate. He made a soft sound in the back of his throat then spun around and hauled her into his arms, pressing her back into the shadows beside Rutherford Ward, his mouth warmly seeking.

'Witch,' he murmured, punctuating the word with tiny, urgent kisses before he captured her entirely. 'You were teasing me. I thought you'd changed your mind.'

'I didn't know what to do,' she protested, kissing him back, weak with relief that he seemed no more sure of how they were to handle this than she was. His vulnerability and his willingness to reveal that to her gave her strength. It reassured her that he didn't see her as a conquest and she needed that reassurance. 'I can't remember the last time anyone held my hand,' she whispered. 'I didn't know what to do.'

'Oh, Maggie.' He lifted her palm and pressed his mouth to it, making her gasp as the touch of him turned her legs weak. 'I want to touch every exquisite inch of you,' he told her fiercely. 'I want to cover you with my mouth and drive us both crazy. I want to make love with you until we're both too exhausted to do anything but sleep.'

She was dizzy. 'And then...?'

'And then I want to wake up and start all over again.' He was still kissing her, short, unbearably wonderful, frustrating kisses that teased her mouth and turned her hot and flushed and desperate for him, giving her the courage to grab at him.

She took his head in her hands, holding him still and forcing him into kissing her properly. 'I want that, too,' she whispered between kisses. 'I've never felt like this before.'

'Come home with me,' he implored. 'Today.'

'Yes.' She bit softly at his lower lip, deepening her caress at his soft groan of response. Neither of them was on call for the day, and although they both made a point of being available for advice if they were needed they were free to leave the hospital after the morning's ICU round. 'I don't even know where you live,' she admitted. He'd invited her to his home more than once but she'd never agreed to go before.

His laugh was soft against her mouth, but the hands that slid beneath her coat to gather her disturbingly to him were firmly determined. 'In town,' he breathed. 'It doesn't matter.'

'You'll have to give me directions.' She kissed his chin, testing the roughness of it against her tongue. 'I'll have to take my car.'

'If that makes you happy.' He pressed her back into the corner at the side of the ward. Hidden from sight, she knew, by the foliage of the Christmas tree, his face flashed briefly red, then pale, then red again from the gleam of the tree's lights.

The top windows were open and above the fresh-washed soapy maleness of Will's skin she could smell the pine's needles. If she closed her eyes she could imagine that they were in a secret forest somewhere.

'Or I could take you,' he said, and she realised he was still talking about his home.

'But then you'd have to bring me all the way back here,' she protested, half holding her breath as her hands sought out the base of his shirt at his back. She made a small sound of appreciation at the warm smoothness of his skin beneath her hands. 'It's so far.'

'You decide.' He was at her mouth again, demanding the response she gave willingly. 'It's academic, anyway,' he groaned, his kiss abruptly hungry. 'I don't think I'm going to be able to let you leave.'

His bleeper was pressed into her thigh and it wasn't so much the sound of it as the vibration that made her realise it was ringing. 'Emergency, Casualty,' it said. 'Emergency, Casualty.'

'I'll come with you,' she gasped quickly, struggling to think. He punched out the security code and then they were inside. If the crisis in Casualty required ICU staff to be called then it probably signified an admission to the unit. It was easier if she knew the details from the start.

They both ran but Will was faster and she got there seconds later. An overweight young man was lying apparently unconscious on a casualty trolley while a worried-looking medical registrar was at the top of the bed, trying to bag him. The discarded ET tube and laryngoscope—the hand-held instrument with a lamp and a blade used for inserting the tube—on the trolley beside them suggested he'd been unable to intubate the patient.

'Nineteen-year-old severe asthmatic,' the registrar told them urgently. 'Respiratory arrest in the ambulance. Neither the cas officer nor I can get the tube down and I'm having a hard job getting any air in here.'

'I'll take over,' Will said quickly, and Maggie saw him nod his thanks when the registrar moved out of the way so that he could take control of the airway. He lifted his patient's chin higher to give a good seal around the mask then turned up the oxygen flow at the wall to the highest possible setting and pumped the bag very gently. 'I need a fresh seven gauge cuffed tube,' he said calmly. 'Get an eight just in case. He's obviously not paralysed. Have you given him any sedation?'

'Nothing,' the registrar said thickly. 'He's not been conscious.'

'Seven here.' The top drawer of the resuscitation trolley held a selection of tubes and Maggie selected the one he wanted. She opened the second drawer down. 'What do you want?'

'Sux and ketamine. He's grossly hyperinflated,' he said

grimly, meaning that his chest was too expanded. While Maggie prepared the muscle relaxant and sedation he'd ordered, Will leaned forward and braced his hands against the boy's ribcage. In a perfectly executed movement he pushed in sharply, forcing some of the air out.

She passed him the syringe then stood back. 'What's in the bag?' she asked, indicating the intravenous drips going into the inside of their patient's right elbow.

'One saline, one salbutamol,' the registrar said promptly. 'Started five minutes ago.'

'Open up the saline,' she instructed.

Will looked up. 'Cricoid pressure, Maggie. I need a humidifier.' He tipped the boy's head back and opened the laryngoscope blade, staring down it while Maggie applied pressure to the boy's broad neck to prevent any reflux of his stomach contents into the lungs if he vomited.

Will had the tube ready and they all fell silent for the few seconds before he muttered triumphantly, 'Got you.'

The tube slid into place. Maggie passed him a ten mil syringe full of air so he could inflate the balloon to seal off the airway around the tube. Working quickly, Will confirmed that the tube was in the right place by listening to the patient's lungs on both sides with his stethoscope. 'Silent chest,' he said grimly. 'His trachea's central. No obvious pneumothorax.'

While he fastened the tube into place with gauze ribbon Maggie controlled the bag, holding the patient steady while Will manually pumped his chest. 'How much adrenaline's he had?'

'Two lots of ten mils of one in a thousand.' The registrar passed her another syringe of it and she gave it to Will to inject through the tube.

'Don't worry about not getting it down,' Maggie heard him tell the registrar quietly. 'He's a big boy and his neck's

very squat. It wasn't easy. You won't come across many
that hard.'

Maggie saw the registrar's immediate relief at Will's
comment and she sent him a grateful look, thanking him
for his customary thoughtfulness.

'Heart rate's still 140.' Maggie watched the cardiac trace
on the monitor beside the bed. Hospital protocol for medical emergencies dictated that the most senior medical doctor present took charge, and although Maggie hadn't been
called to come she was the only physician present and as
such she automatically became the designated leader. 'Any
blood pressure?'

'I can't find anything,' one of the nurses said urgently.
'The machine can't either.'

'I've got a weak carotid pulse,' Maggie said crisply, her
fingers at the young man's neck. 'He needs a decent line.
Will…?'

'Internal jugular,' he said immediately, already swabbing
the neck as if he'd sensed her command before she'd even
voiced it. He gloved and held out his hand for the line the
registrar had ready for him.

Maggie took over and very slowly and gently bagged
their patient, relieved to feel that there was less resistance
than there'd been at first. Obviously Will's chest decom-
pressions, in combination with the medication, were achiev-
ing something. The trick in severe asthma was to deliberately under-ventilate because part of the pathology was that
the lungs contained too much air already.

She didn't bother to watch Will with the line—he could
do that sort of thing in his sleep. 'We need a gas,' she told
the registrar.

'Right away.' He unwrapped one of the pre-heparinised
syringes used for checking the blood gas levels. 'Femoral
artery OK?'

'Anywhere.' She kept her eye on the monitor. 'Switch

the salbutamol across into the central line,' she instructed, as soon as it was in place and Will had taken over bagging again. 'We need an adrenaline infusion. Twenty milligrams in 500 mils of 5 per cent dextrose on a pump, please. Someone put a bottle of bicarb up now.'

'Bicarb going in.' The casualty officer punctured a bottle, running it through a line into the vein in the patient's arm while the nurse went for the adrenaline.

'Has he had any steroids?' Maggie asked. 'What's he on for his asthma?'

'Maintenance five milligrams of steroid, nebulised Ventolin when required and no other oral stuff,' a nurse told her, reading notes.

'We hadn't got around to giving him any steroid yet,' the registrar added.

'Hydrocortisone 350 milligrams i.v. stat,' Maggie ordered. 'Do we know why he went off?'

'According to the ambulance guys, he'd been at a beach party with a bonfire,' the casualty officer told her. 'It was pretty smoky. He's been wheezy the last few weeks and in Hutt hospital for two nights a week ago, but it sounds as if the bonfire might have been the critical bit.'

She nodded. 'Will, is anything happening?'

'He's not so tight.' He moved his hand so she could see the bag he was pumping. 'We're going to have to keep this up.'

'Adrenaline ready,' a nurse announced. She turned the pump so Maggie could see it. 'What rate shall I set?'

Maggie mentally calculated the boy's approximate weight, punched in a moderately high dose to start and pushed the button to start the pump.

'Gases are through.' Another nurse came running back with the test the registrar had taken. She handed the results to Maggie who checked them, noting—but not especially worried by—the high level of carbon dioxide before passing them to Will.

'Carotid pulse is stronger,' Will said, his hand on the boy's neck.

'I've got a blood pressure,' the nurse who'd brought the adrenaline announced, lifting her head from where she'd been listening at the boy's arm. 'Ninety over seventy.'

'Well done.' Maggie felt herself start to relax. 'Good. How's his air entry?'

'Improving.' Will looked up from his chest with a quick smile. 'Let's try him with a nebuliser.'

Once that was bubbling, and things appeared stable, Maggie went to call the unit to explain that they'd be coming up. 'We'll ventilate him probably a couple of days at least,' she told the registrar when she returned.

In England, in her experience, she'd only very rarely ventilated an asthmatic patient—their drive to breathe was normally extremely strong—but even the short time she'd spent in New Zealand had changed her opinion on such things. Wellington's surrounds had one of the world's highest rates of severe asthma and she was much more wary now of under-treating. 'We need an X-ray before transfer.'

'The radiographer is already here,' someone told her, and she turned around and saw her waiting.

'Go straight in,' Maggie instructed, standing back. 'One AP is fine for now but we might need some more films upstairs.'

Someone would have to stay to bag their patient during the X-ray, and there was a lead apron slung across the large arm of the machine which would protect that person from the radiation, but Will's ICU bleeper sounded just as they were manoeuvring into position and so Maggie took the apron for herself.

'You go,' she told him firmly, lifting the heavy garment over her head before she took over the bag he'd been squeezing, her mouth drying at the firm brush of his body as they changed places and he moved out from behind her. 'See what they want. I'll finish everything here.'

'I'll see you upstairs,' he said quietly, the warmth of his regard reminding her suddenly that on all the occasions they'd had to perform a similar swap in the past he'd never, ever, touched her like that.

'OK.' Knowing she was flushing, she lowered her head quickly, abruptly shy. It was barely twelve hours since he'd come back from Sydney yet he'd turned her life inside out. What would happen when they made love?

CHAPTER NINE

WILL's bleeper asked him to call ICU but as he was already in the building he simply went up there. Steven was at the main desk. 'Sorry, Tim took the call from Dr Miller just before so I didn't get a chance to ask her about this,' he said, walking in front of him to Mrs Everett's bed. 'I know you weren't planning on bringing her around this quickly but she's not liking the tube. She's breathing on her own so, rather than sedating her again, I thought it best to check with you first.'

'Taking it out sounds like a good idea,' Will said quietly, checking her results. Earlier, he'd switched the ventilator so that it waited for her to take a breath first, rather than pushing the air into her lungs—only taking over if she didn't take a breath. It seemed she'd been breathing on her own for most of the night.

'How's her BP?'

'Stable all night.' Her nurse pointed out the readings she'd charted. 'No problems. She's been making signals, asking about the baby. Her husband's still in Wellington with the little one.'

In answer to Will's quick look she said, 'No, it's all right. She's fine. They're still happy.'

'Do you hear that, Mrs Everett?' He nodded at her. Obviously still fairly drowsy, she opened her eyes slowly but he saw that she heaved a little against the tube. Will introduced himself. 'You won't remember now but I was your anaesthetist when you had your baby last night. That tube in your mouth's annoying you, is it?'

She nodded weakly, lifting one hand in apparent confirmation, and he nodded to Steven. 'It can come out,' he told him, 'but cover her with the hydralazine in case her BP goes up as you do it.'

Mrs Adams's results looked marginally improved. It was very early days and the course of ARDS rarely ran smoothly or predictably but her oxygen levels had improved without further increase in the concentration from the seventy-five per cent she'd needed earlier and that was a very positive sign.

Her husband was still asleep in the chair by her side but he woke when Will crouched to listen to his wife's lungs. 'It's all right,' he said soothingly. 'She's a little better.'

Maggie arrived with an orderly and a nurse and their new admission as Will was finishing his brief round, and he and Tim went to help. Not that he had any doubts about Maggie's ability to settle their new patient in, he admitted. It was simply that the sooner they could finish here the sooner he could take her away again.

'Keep up the ketamine?' she ventured. 'What do you think?'

'Seems appropriate,' he agreed softly.

'I haven't used an air-bed as he should only be here a short time,' Tim told them as they prepared to transfer. 'Should we use leg pumps with him?'

'Fine.' Will held their patient up on his side so that the nurse could slide a transfer board underneath him. The automatically inflating leg rings had been shown to reduce the risk of formation of blood clots in patients' legs during ICU stays, and he was happy to use them in this case. He lowered their patient back onto the board and they slid it across to the bed and repeated the procedure. 'How was the X-ray?'

'Nothing unexpected.' Maggie was controlling the patient's head through the move. 'Asthma. No infection.' She started transferring connections from the portable machine to one of the unit ventilators. 'His gases are good. His serum potassium is low but all other bloods are fine. White count is normal but high eosinophils.'

He nodded. Eosinophils were the particular kind of white blood cell which reacted in allergic-type conditions such as asthma. 'Do we have any family?'

'No one yet. One of his friends at the party told the ambulance crew that his mum and dad and the other children have gone away camping for the holidays. Apparently, they usually put the caravan on the ferry and head across to Nelson.' She'd stepped back to allow him to take over at the machine. 'The police are chasing them up.'

'Nothing else in Casualty?'

'It's very quiet.' The student nurse who'd come with Maggie from Casualty was handing over to Tim but she sent him a warm, very friendly smile. 'We're not expecting anything else,' she added.

'Good.' He returned her smile easily and thoughtlessly, then out of the corner of his eye caught the sharp look his smile had provoked from Maggie, apparently not busy enough herself checking the infusions to have missed the exchange.

He stilled, watching her, his awareness rewarded by the quick intake of breath which lifted her chest and betrayed the emotion he knew she was trying to conceal before she seemed to turn her attention very deliberately back to her work.

The casualty nurse, though, had apparently noticed nothing amiss because she was still smiling at him. 'If it's still quiet we're having a champagne breakfast in Cas at handover. The day staff will only have a sip or two so there'll be plenty spare. There's room for everyone and afterwards we're having drinks at my flat. We'll have loads of fun. Please come.'

Amused, he noted that she held his gaze far longer than

she should have, before including the charge nurse in her invitation. 'You, too, of course. Everyone's welcome.'

Will took care not to look at Maggie who, he could tell, was working very hard at pretending disinterest despite the fact that he could feel her watchfulness around him like a blanket. 'Thank you…' he checked the name badge she wore prominently displayed '…Jacqueline. That's very kind but—'

'Jacky,' she said quickly.

'Jacky.' He smiled. 'But I won't be coming. I don't know about Tim…'

'Sorry.' Tim looked definitely wary now and he sent Will a telling look which suggested he wasn't impressed about being included. 'Not after a double shift like this. And it's chaos around here at hand-over. It takes hours sometimes. But thanks.'

Tim disconnected the salbutamol and adrenaline infusions from the pumps the nurse had brought up from Casualty, swapping them to ICU pumps before guiding both casualty nurse and casualty pumps to the door. 'Thanks, Jacky. Merry Christmas. Have a good party.'

Maggie was at the chart now, still so studiously avoiding his gaze that Will couldn't hold back his smile. 'I can't believe you're jealous,' he teased softly.

'I don't know what you're talking about,' she said crisply, each word perfectly enunciated. 'He's allergic to penicillin. I saw it in his old notes. I'll write it in red here.'

'I only smiled at her.' Coming so unexpectedly, he found her possessiveness enchanting. 'Frankly, she's not remotely my type.'

'Frankly, I'm not remotely interested.' She still wouldn't look at him. 'According to the old notes, he's been admitted twice in the past into ICU in Wellington. The first time he was ventilated overnight, the second time for three days.

No problems weaning. No ICU admissions for the past year and a half.'

'Maggie, this is in your imagination.'

'It makes no difference to me, Will.' He saw a small movement at her throat, as if she was swallowing heavily, but when she lifted her head her expression was calm and her eyes fiercely and frustratingly guarded.

'Phew!' Tim was back and he grinned at them and mock-wiped the back of his hand across his forehead. 'That woman is a man-eater,' he announced dramatically, prompting Will to send Maggie an I-told-you-so look which she flatly refused to acknowledge.

'She's only just out of training, for goodness' sake,' Tim continued, reading whatever Maggie had written on the chart over her shoulder. 'Whatever happened to those little shy nurses we all were when I first graduated? We were too timid to even ask anyone more senior if we could have two minutes off to get to the loo, and now here they are, asking the doctors and charge nurses out for breakfast. What next?'

'Next is our patient,' Maggie said pointedly, looking at him. 'Finished socialising and ready for work, Charge Nurse?'

'Yes.' Will suppressed a smile as the younger man, not appearing remotely abashed, beamed at her. 'Go, Dr Miller. Hit me with it. I'm all ears.'

'Two hourly humidified nebulised salbutamol on oxygen, four-hourly 350 mg hydrocortisone, i.v. salbutamol as I've charted. Let's reduce the adrenaline slightly, continue sedation and add in routine ulcer prevention.'

Will waited quietly while she ran through the ventilator settings they wanted in the way they always did with each new case, agreeing with the volumes and timings she chose.

With asthma it was important to maintain a constant volume of warm, humidified air with each breath, at the same time programming a low breathing rate. This allowed a long time for the patient to breathe out because in this disease the lungs were already very well inflated. The problem was getting that air out again through the inflamed and narrowed airways. PEEP, so important to Mrs Adams, was almost contraindicated.

'We'll definitely be keeping him ventilated today,' Maggie finished. 'We won't have any problems weaning him when we need to. He's young and his breathing drive will be strong.'

'So no Christmas lunch,' Tim said cheerfully, noting down the details of what she'd said. 'He won't be missing much. It's only roast mutton today.'

Will sent him a sharp look. 'I thought Christmas meant turkey and trimmings?'

'Too expensive this year,' Tim said sternly, rolling his eyes. 'Well, roast turkey was, at least. I heard they were allowed to do turkey fricassee, which is apparently some sort of awful casserole with a thick white sauce and sweet-corn, but the cooks decided that a roast was a better alternative. They're doing potatoes and pumpkin and peas and there's proper pudding or trifle for dessert. The kitchen staff's trying hard. It shouldn't be too bad.'

'Better than dry cheese sandwiches, which is all we got last year,' Maggie said thinly, still, Will registered, seeming to be avoiding any eye contact with him. 'Remember, Tim?'

'All I remember from last Christmas is those five over-dose admissions and the two great pile-ups on the motor-way.' The nurse tapped the metal bed-frame. 'Touch wood, so far it's been a happy holiday in here for us.'

He looked up then as if to utter some sort of religious praise but instead he simply blinked, his eyes going to the windows above them. 'Lord!' he said starkly. 'It's light already. What time is it?'

'Five.' Maggie was bent over, writing in the notes, but she glanced at her watch.

'I'd better get moving,' Tim announced. 'Back in a sec.'

Will himself was surprised by the time. The night had been eventful enough to have seemed extraordinarily brief. Maggie was signing her name very neatly but very slowly at the bottom of her admission account. He bided his time until she'd finished then said, 'I've seen everyone else here. He's fine now. Steven's here to watch things. Let's go.'

'Go where?'

'Out of here,' he said strongly. He took her hand, even though he knew she didn't want him now, simply because he couldn't not touch her for another minute while he talked her around. 'Now.'

He spoke very quietly, even though the only person who could possibly have overheard him was behind them now and deeply sedated. 'I'm going slowly mad. The only cure is to kiss you.'

She sent him an uncertain look but she let him hustle her out of the unit although she wrenched her hand away once the doors swung closed on the hand-washing area. 'I wasn't finished,' she said shortly.

'Any more finished and you'd have been drawing pictures,' he observed, amused. Once he'd washed he dried his hands on a paper towel and bent to press a kiss to the enchanting curve of her neck where she stood bent slightly over the basin. 'How could you let that girl bother you like that? You know I'm not interested in her.'

'How am I supposed to know which ones you are and aren't interested in?' She dodged away from him to dry her hands. 'Given that you seem to be offered such an abundant choice.'

He was pleased, at least, that she wasn't trying to deny that he was right about the reasons behind her change of mood but, still, it astonished him that she thought there could be room in his head for any woman but her. Despite the easy way she'd revealed her husband's infidelity, perhaps her scars went deeper than she wanted him to see. 'She's young,' he said dismissively, understanding that she needed reassurance.

'She was very pretty.'

'She's *too* young.'

'I didn't think she appeared particularly unsophisticated.'

'Cat.' He laughed at that. 'I think I like you being jealous. It brings out a whole new side of your nature.'

'I'm not jealous.' She passed him his white coat and collected her own from the hook next to it. 'It just makes me thoughtful.'

But the thought of her being thoughtful unnerved him and he frowned. Thoughtful meant she might be rational and that meant second thoughts and he didn't like that. He wanted her aroused and emotional. Now that he'd felt how she could be when she was willing he could no longer bear the thought of her changing her mind.

'Thoughtful?' he echoed, keeping his tone deliberately teasing while he tugged her into his arms. 'That sounds far too serious for a beautiful Christmas Day morning.' He lowered his mouth, his back to the doors to protect her in case they opened. 'Has anyone ever told you that you have the most beautiful mouth in the world?'

'No.' Her soft voice had a husky edge which delighted him. 'Will...'

'Shush.' Lost now, too close to her, he realised his assumption that he could control her like this was ludicrous because he couldn't even control himself. She set him on fire.

He took her mouth, unable to stop himself, and gently ravaged it until they were both breathing quickly. If she hadn't heard something, hadn't stiffened and pulled back, he knew that he could have made love to her there in that room regardless of the fact that there was a ward of patients and nine nurses less than five metres away behind loosely swinging doors.

He let her go reluctantly and she wrenched herself out of his arms and spun back to the basins, as if trying to pretend that she was still washing her hands when Tim came hurtling in.

'Oh, good, you're still here,' he gasped. 'Thought I might catch you.' If he thought there was anything odd about them still being there together his cheerful expression didn't reveal it. He held out a chart towards them. 'Mrs Adams's gentamicin. I see you reduced her dose last night. When do you want us to re-check her levels? Steven wasn't sure.'

'Nine tonight,' Maggie told him, her expression, Will saw, perfectly controlled although it pleased him to see the hand she stretched out to take the chart still trembled. She drew a little box around the place on the chart where the evening's dose would be recorded, the agreed symbol in the unit for the time to check blood levels. 'Sorry. I should have remembered to do this.'

'Not a problem,' Tim said cheerfully. 'See you later.'

When the doors swung shut again behind the nurse, Will put his arm around Maggie's shoulders. He guided her away from the unit but at the door into the hospital corridor she dodged his arm and went ahead of him. When he went to take her hand she put it behind her back, as if that would keep him away.

'Not now,' she said softly, sending him a warning look. 'Someone might see.'

He walked on a few paces, digesting that, then stopped abruptly, telling himself that it wasn't hurt that compelled him but simply curiosity. 'It's five in the morning and the corridor is deserted,' he said quietly. 'Suppose you tell me what you really mean.'

'What I mean is that here is not the right place.' Her voice quivered slightly but she sounded determined enough.

'By here you mean this corridor in particular?'

'I mean anywhere where we might be seen.' She sounded exasperated although he had no idea why. 'Five seconds earlier and Tim would have seen us.'

Will shook his head slowly, not understanding. 'Tim's unshockable,' he said easily. 'Can't you tell? He's seen it all. Don't worry about him.'

'I'm not worrying about him,' she countered, sending him a puzzled look which told him nothing. 'I meant we wouldn't want him to think we were more than simply colleagues.'

'Wouldn't we?' He studied her blankly.

'We don't want anyone to guess.'

'Guess what?'

'Will!'

He frowned. 'Are you saying that it matters to you what people think?'

'Of course it matters to me.'

She was staring at him as if his question had bewildered her, but to him it hadn't been anything other than genuine. 'It's not as if they're not going to find out eventually,' he said heavily. 'I'm not going to sneak around, pretending we're not lovers—'

'What?' To his astonishment she looked appalled. 'What do you mean, you're not going to pretend? You mean you really do want everyone to know?'

'I don't care who knows.' He didn't understand why they were arguing or even what they were arguing about. As far as he was concerned, who knew or didn't know what was totally immaterial to either of them.

'Do you see me as some sort of trophy you're going to be able to boast about?'

'Of course not.'

'I suppose now you're going to tell me that Jeremy Donaldson's going to find out about this?'

'Jeremy?' He blinked at her, bemused. 'Maggie, Jeremy and his wife are friends of mine. There'll be times when we see them together. Of course they'll know. They'll guess even if we don't tell them.'

'I don't believe this.'

Her incredulity was genuine, he realised. For reasons beyond his comprehension she seemed to find the prospect of both mixing with his friends and revealing their relationship horrifying.

He reached for her. 'Maggie…?'

But a crashing noise sent her springing away. There was a bank of lifts around from the short end of the corridor and the crash must have been one of the lift doors opening because seconds later a whistling porter in a red Father Christmas hat wheeled a trolley around the corner. 'Morning, Doctors.' His grin was cheerful as he came past. 'Lovely day for it.'

'Morning,' they echoed, and Will added, 'Merry Christmas.'

'See what I mean?' Maggie had avoided looking at him until the other man had passed. 'Look what almost happened again. This is impossible.'

'Just explain to me what is so awful about someone catching me kissing you,' he said quietly, striving for patience when what he really wanted to do was take her in his arms and kiss her senseless.

'The awful bit for me comes next week,' she said fiercely.

'Next week,' he echoed hollowly, acknowledging that he was now completely and irretrievably flummoxed. 'What happens next week?'

'Tomorrow, then,' she said sharply.

'Tomorrow?' He fell silent, staring at her. Flushed and

shaking, her lovely hair coming loose from its knot, her achingly enchanting eyes wide and sparkling with a hurt he didn't understand, she was the most beautiful, desirable woman he'd ever seen in his life—but he had no idea what she was talking about.

'Oh, Will, I've been there before,' she said eventually. 'I told you what happened with Graham at the end, about how everybody knew about him and Rebecca. I hated that. I hated pretending that I didn't mind. I was only four months through a six-month job and I couldn't leave. People were very nice but it didn't help. I still knew they were all feeling sorry for me and it was awful.'

Finally he had a glimmer of understanding. 'That wouldn't happen,' he said slowly. 'I promise. Trust me, Maggie. I'm not like your husband.'

'Who you are or aren't like is immaterial,' she said softly. 'You and I are talking about…sex.' She hesitated enchantingly over the word, her lower lip puckering slightly as she worried it briefly with her teeth, but she continued more strongly, 'About an affair, not about marriage. It won't last for ever so it's inevitable the same situation will arise. I'm simply saying that it would be much easier for me if we just kept this between ourselves.'

'Because you're worried what people will say when it ends?'

'Exactly.' Perhaps relieved that he seemed to finally understand, she half smiled at him, obviously unaware of the surge of irritation her words had provoked in him. 'It's different for a man,' she explained. 'They seem to get some sort of bizarre kudos from something like that. But people always feel sorry for the woman.'

He tried to stay patient. 'Maggie, it doesn't make sense to go into a relationship, already thinking about it ending.'

'I think it makes perfect sense,' she countered. Her little chin came up with a defensiveness that made him curl his fists into his sides as he fought the abrupt desire to ravish her. 'I'm being practical.'

'Then don't be,' he ground out. He didn't want her to be practical. He didn't want her to think about when their relationship ended. He wanted her thinking about it beginning. He wanted her to be obsessed, like him—now—when all he could think about was how it was going to be when they made love.

'Don't tell me what to do,' she said jerkily.

'You're being ridiculous,' he protested.

'I don't have to listen to this.' Her flashing eyes betraying an intensity of anger he'd never seen in her before, he stood suddenly spellbound while she whirled away from him. 'You're the one being ridiculous,' she raged. 'Ridiculous and manipulative and…and… You just want me to stick my head in the sand and let you walk all over me. Well, just forget it. That's never going to happen. You're never going to sweep me off my feet, Will Saunders, because my feet are staying right here on the ground.'

He moved fast, caught her and pressed her against the wall of the corridor, not caring if they were seen, careless now of anyone but her. 'Our first fight,' he said thickly, his mouth at her throat. 'I love it.'

'You love fighting?' The words were tiny, hoarse whispers against his cheek, but she wasn't resisting him.

'I love seeing you angry.' He kissed her mouth. 'I love you being fierce and emotional.' His voice rough, he captured her earlobe gently between his teeth. 'But it doesn't happen often enough.' He bent slightly to slide his arm beneath her knees and lifted her into his arms. She was light and delicate and unbelievably desirable. 'I'm sweeping you off your feet,' he teased, sure of himself now. 'Is that all right?'

'Mmm.' She pressed urgent little kisses to his chin. 'Where are we going?'

'Somewhere private.' He carried her to the lifts, kissing her and nuzzling her mouth as they waited for one to open. Once inside he let her down but not out of his arms. 'Have I told you yet how desirable you are this morning, Dr Miller?'

'Have I told you yet how prickly you are this morning, Dr Saunders?'

Will raised his head, saw the red traces he'd left against the pale skin of her face and neck and winced. 'Sorry.' He stroked her face with one tender finger then ran an assessing hand beneath his chin and grimaced at the contrast. 'My suitcase with my shaving gear is in the car. I guess I'd better pick it up on the way over.'

'I don't mind.' Her eyes were shy. 'I find it…sexy.'

'Sexy, hmm?' Immediately fully aroused again, he gathered her completely into his arms and captured the sweet, startled laugh that escaped her, taking care not to hurt her with the roughness of his skin. 'I'll show you sexy.' The press of her breasts at his chest was driving him wild and he pushed her coat apart and hauled up her top.

'This,' he growled, 'is sexy.'

The brush of the warmed tightness of her against his mouth sent him halfway to heaven. She was exquisite. He was greedy suddenly. He wanted everything. He lifted her, taking the full weight of her into his arms to better taste her breasts, and fell back against one corner of the lift, hitting the back of his head but not caring, careless again of anything but her.

She was soft and she was willing and he'd never felt anything so good in his life.

The lift stopped somewhere, but the doors didn't open and he punched blindly at the panel to send them rising again.

'Will…?' Her small gasp and the gentle, urgent movements of her hands at his head brought him back slightly.

His muscles clenched in sudden protest but she wasn't telling him to stop. 'I can't touch you,' she protested, her voice above him but muffled by the gathered fabric of her top around his face. 'Your shirt…'

'It doesn't matter.' But impatiently he lifted it. He slid it between her body and his, tensing at the light brush of her breasts against his bared flesh as she moved to embrace him. Moistened by his tongue, the damp press of her nipples was coolly exquisite against his own heated flesh, and he bent swiftly and captured them again, teasing her with flickering licks of his tongue in retaliation for the teasing, hesitant brush of her hands across his chest.

The lift stopped again—somewhere up top, he thought—and he stabbed at the panel again to start them moving, not caring. It was an isolated bank, used only for moving equipment and ICU and theatre patients and staff, and it was too early for there to be any demand for them. But even if it hadn't been, despite his promise to her to keep this secret, he acknowledged, right then, with her half-naked and in his arms, he wouldn't have cared.

'Oh…help.' Her eyes were half-closed and she tipped her head back, allowing him access to the pinkened delicious curve of her throat. 'This is insane.'

Then the lift lurched downwards a floor and that seemed to startle her. She reached out to brace herself, her palms going flat against opposite walls of the corner. 'No, stop,' she protested vaguely, arching her body away from him when he tried to bring her back again. 'We have to wait. I feel as if I'll explode if you touch me again.'

'Then let me touch you,' he groaned, reaching for her. Her top had slipped down again, covering her breasts when he wanted her bare.

She closed her eyes, panting, then started to come back to him, but the lift jerked to a stop and they both heard the chime that signalled the opening of the doors. She screamed a little, shocking him—shocking them both, he saw from her expression—and he went instinctively forward to shield her, searching for the button that would keep the doors closed, but he was too late.

CHAPTER TEN

THERE was no one there. It was quite dim. There was some furniture stacked in front of the lift and four or five huge enclosed steel trolleys lined up, which suggested that a porter had been waiting at least, but perhaps he'd gone looking for more trolleys because there was no sign of him.

Maggie didn't know what to do. She was hot and flushed and her breasts ached and her nipples felt like tiny wounds on her chest, hurting with the smallest lifting movement of her breath against her top. Really, all Will had done was kiss her and caress her breasts yet she felt like she'd been through a cyclone.

Dizzily, she stepped out, blinking vaguely, aware of Will behind her but too appalled at the thought of what he must be thinking of her to look at him. She'd only just finished warning him to keep his hands off her in public, but after that...

Shocked by her wantonness, sure that he must be convinced by now that she was some sort of frustrated nymphomaniac, she was too embarrassed to turn around. How could she possibly explain that that *abandon* wasn't her normal behaviour? Who would believe her? The evidence so far that night had been pretty strongly to the contrary. As far as Will went, it seemed that if he touched her she melted.

She wound her way out between the trolleys and peered between the needled branches of the decorated Christmas tree, which someone had left perched against the wall, so that she could read the listing of the floors and work out where they were. Gingerly, she inspected the corridor on either side of the bank of lifts. 'We're in the basement,' she told him. Her voice sounded as if someone had scratched sandpaper across it. 'The stairs are just here. Shall we walk up?'

'I'll catch you up.' His voice sounded almost as rough as hers, and when she turned back he was sitting on one of the chairs by the lift, leaning forward, his arms braced on his knees.

She swallowed heavily. 'Will…?'

He lifted his head slowly, but to her relief where she'd half expected shock or disgust at her behaviour his regard was reassuringly warm. 'Unless you want to come here and do something about how I'm feeling right now,' he said dryly, 'it's going to take me a few more minutes to recover.'

'Oh.' She lowered her head quickly, her embarrassment immediately doubling. 'I'm sorry.'

'It's not your fault,' he murmured. 'Well, at least it *is* your fault but I don't mind.' He sounded amused. 'I'll only be a minute or two. I'll collect my things from my car and meet you at your flat.'

It took her longer than normal to find her way home. It wasn't far, but her head wasn't working properly and she got confused, getting out of the basement and into the right part of the main block. As far as the actual walking went, her legs felt like floppy pegs.

She went straight for her shower, hoping that the cool spray might help cool the blood that still pumped hotly through her veins. Leaving her bleeper where she could get to it on the edge of the basin, she stripped, grabbed her shampoo, released her hair and stepped beneath the water, automatically muttering her usual mental plea for her bleeper to stay silent long enough for her to wash.

As it was such a warm morning, rather than attempting

to style her hair she blotted it with a towel and left it to dry naturally. She scrubbed her teeth then fastened another towel around herself above her breasts, gathered up her discarded clothes and headed for her bedroom.

She came up short at the sight of Will, sprawled across her unmade bed, feet lazily crossed at his ankles, but it seemed that she was the only one who found anything awkward about the moment because he simply levered himself up, collected a sponge bag he must have brought from his car, pressed a quick kiss to the top of her head and wandered past her into her bathroom.

'I need a shave before I shower,' he said easily. He'd left the door a little ajar and she heard water filling the basin. 'How was the water?'

'Fine.' Bemused by the casual intimacy of their exchange, she hadn't moved. This felt extremely strange, she realised. *Extremely* strange. Perhaps it was just that she'd grown so used to living alone that any change from that even for one day would shake her, or perhaps it was just that it was Will.

Will Saunders was in her bathroom. *Her* bathroom. And when he'd finished showering he was probably expecting to come to her bedroom and make love to her.

The reality of that sucked every little molecule of the fragile self-assurance she'd managed to scrape together right back out of her again and she sank onto the bed soundlessly. Will was going to make love to her.

It seemed extraordinary. It had been the most incredible night of her life. She was going to go to bed with Will. She *wanted* to go to bed with Will and *it was going to happen.*

When he came back to the bedroom, his hair and body still damp from the shower, she realised she must have been sitting there for quite some time. The towel was still her only covering and put her hand over the knot to hold it in position.

'I don't have any contraception,' she said baldly.

'I don't either so we'll have to wait,' he said evenly, not appearing to be particularly bothered.

'It's Christmas Day. There'll only be a few shops open this morning.'

'Leave it to me.'

He had a yellow towel wound around his waist and when he crouched at a small case near the window the towel parted along the line of one muscled thigh and she averted her eyes, swallowing. 'Will...I hardly know you.'

'You know me well enough.' The narrowed sideways look he sent her was amused. 'Come on, Maggie,' he chided gently. 'It's been almost a year.'

'Do you have a girlfriend?' At his startled look she said quickly, 'It's a serious question. I mean, I don't even know. Are you...seeing anybody?'

'No.'

'Even casually, I mean. Like us, for instance. Anyone like...like that?'

'No.' He straightened slowly. 'And I wouldn't use the word ''casual'' in reference to our relationship.'

She moistened her lips, her mouth painfully dry. 'I find it hard to believe you're not involved with anyone. You're a very attractive man. I'm curious about why you're not married.'

'I'm not married and I'm not involved with any woman at the moment but you.' He hadn't moved away from the case but he felt much closer now. 'Why are you doing this?'

'I'm not doing anything.'

'You're erecting barriers between us,' he said strongly. 'If you're having second thoughts, tell me so that we can deal with them. Don't simply create problems where there are none.'

'How do I know there are none? You know everything about me and I still know hardly anything about you.'

'OK.' He smiled. 'OK, that's fine. Tell me what you want to know.'

'Why aren't you married?'

'That's not a mystery.' Still smiling and still wearing his towel, he came to the bed and stretched out behind her on his side. She let him pull her back so she sat against him, her hip in the curve of his body and one arm supporting herself behind him. 'I'm difficult,' he said quietly. 'And I've never met a woman I've wanted to marry.'

'But you've had relationships?' she said huskily.

'A couple long-term,' he acknowledged. 'Some shorter.'

'Jeremy said something about a doctor in London.'

'I've told you before to forget anything Jeremy says,' he chided. He'd gathered the damp ends of her hair in his hand and now he was stroking them, running them through his fingers. 'Is that why you wouldn't go out with me?'

She didn't answer that. It had bothered her, of course, but her reasons for not accepting any of his invitations had been far more complex than simple concern about another woman. 'He made it sound serious,' she said huskily.

'You don't get to my age without having had a few serious relationships,' he answered soberly. 'And I did live with someone in London but it didn't last. My...head was never involved. She's met someone since I left. She wrote recently. She sounds happy.'

'Your head was never involved,' she said softly, liking that.

His eyes had gone dark. 'Do you understand what it means?'

'Of course.' It was what she felt now, she realised. This total...taking over of her mind until it was filled with him.

'What sort of woman are you looking for? What sort of woman do you want to marry?'

'Someone like my mother,' he said slowly, his smile turning immediately rueful when she couldn't hide her re-action to that. 'Witch,' he cursed, burrowing into her towel-covered stomach with his face while she laughed. 'This is not anything sinister or Freudian. I've just grown up seeing how happy my father's been.'

'That's sick,' she protested. 'You've studied psychiatry. How can you possibly say something like that with a straight face?'

'Not just my mother. Catherine, Jeremy's wife, has the same sort of personality,' he said lightly. 'Those sorts of women always seem to have contented husbands.'

'But Jeremy's not contented. I've never met anyone more miserable.'

'It's all an act,' he argued. 'He perfected it at primary school. He wants everyone to feel sorry for him so they give him an easy time. He's supremely contented with his home life. Catherine manages everything—he doesn't need to even think about it.'

'Catherine,' she repeated, wondering. 'Will—'

'No,' he said firmly, one finger closing her mouth. 'Not even remotely. Never in my life. I was best man at their wedding, for heaven's sake.'

'But you want someone just like her?'

'Someone practical and cheerful,' he agreed. 'Someone who'll be happy, staying at home and bringing up loads of children. Someone who doesn't have crises and isn't neurotic. Someone who manages everything so I can get on with my work.'

'I need someone like that,' she said faintly.

His laugh was warm against her stomach. 'She sounds pretty good, doesn't she?'

'Amazing,' Maggie admitted. 'I'm beginning to understand why you're still single. You know I'm hardly ever cheerful?'

'I've noticed that.'

'I have loads of crises and I'm highly neurotic.'

'But you have great legs,' he said reassuringly, sliding back her towel and inspecting her thighs. 'Wonderful legs.'

'When you say *loads* of children…?'

'Two at least.' He lifted the towel high enough to make her push it hastily back down again. 'Why? Don't you want them?'

'Two at most,' she said thickly. 'Plus a full-time nanny. I couldn't bear not to work. Will…?'

He probed at the towel. 'Mmm?'

Maggie held on tight. 'You want all of this in a woman and your head involved as well?'

'I think I'm going to end up compromising on the head bit,' he muttered, moving sideways so that her head fell back onto the bed, his face intent on the part of her she was determined to keep firmly concealed by the towel. 'The head bit's too disturbing.' He pressed a hard, achingly sensual kiss to the inner part of one of her thighs. 'I don't think I like it. Maggie, let go.'

'No.' Rigid with shyness, she held on tight. 'Stop it.'

'Let me look. I won't hurt you. I just want to look.'

'Absolutely not.' Shaking, she jackknifed off the bed. 'You're shameless.'

'And you're so shy.' He looked entranced. 'Come back.'

'Not in a million years.' She re-tightened the towel, binding it very firmly around her breasts, relieved that for the moment he wasn't intending to pursue her. Although her shock was real, her resistance wasn't as strong as she'd expected it to be. 'I have to get dressed.' She was ready, willing, to have sex with him, she told herself. But later when they were properly prepared. What he'd wanted then was far too…intimate for her to be comfortable with right now.

'What about the unit?' She opened her wardrobe. 'They've been very quiet.' She was talking quickly now. 'Do you think you should give Tim or Steven a call?'

'Tim's never shy about bleeping us,' he said lazily. Stretched out now with his arms folded casually behind his head, he was watching her with sleepy interest. 'Wear the blue one,' he advised. 'When you bend forward in that I can see your breasts.'

Horrified, she pulled the dress, one of her favourites, from its hanger and threw it into the depths of the cupboard. 'I'm going to wear my tracksuit,' she said sharply, selecting the high-necked, red, fluffy-cotton outfit. 'The colour's seasonal.'

She snatched some underwear from her bottom drawer, then turned back to him and hesitated, clutching her clothes to her chest. 'When do I bend forward?'

'At your desk. When you're writing notes. When you're checking reflexes,' he said quietly. 'When you're intubating. Sometimes you put the staffroom's newspaper on the floor and lean over to read it. Times like that.'

'But I wear that dress all the time.'

'Not all the time,' he said quietly. 'But I wish you would. You were wearing it the first time I saw you and I fell in love with it.'

'I can't believe you've never warned me,' she choked, still aghast. 'How many other people have noticed—'

'I've never caught anyone else looking, and if they had been I would have,' he said shortly. 'It's not so obvious. I just happen to have always found it difficult not to look at you.'

'What other clothes should I worry about?'

'Your white blouse with the short sleeves is see-through when you're against the light.'

'Against the light,' she echoed numbly.

'By bed twelve with the window behind you on a sunny day,' he amended. 'Last time you weren't wearing anything under it Ian and Tim and I just about had heart attacks.'

'Will!'

'All right, all right, it's totally unprofessional and an insult to your position and I'm sorry,' he said, but he was laughing. 'Maggie, it's not our fault that you happen to have fantastic breasts,' he protested, curling up when she hit him with a flying dress. 'Men notice those sorts of things.'

'*Perverts* notice those sorts of things,' she hissed, outraged. 'This is unbelievable.'

'Give me some credit.' He was still laughing. 'At least I'm telling you now.'

'And why is that exactly?' she demanded. 'Because you want me to wear something even worse that you're not telling me about?'

'I'm telling you because you're mine now.' Moving too quickly for her to get away he surged from the bed and caught her against him, his kiss immediately and fiercely demanding. 'I don't want anyone else looking.'

'I'm not *yours*,' she panted, wriggling free when he lifted his head and retreating smartly towards the bathroom, clothes in hand. His possessiveness, coming so unexpectedly, suddenly terrified her. 'I'm mine. Just because we're going to have sex once or twice doesn't mean you can start turning all caveman.'

'Once or twice?' He laughed out loud. 'Is that a joke?'

'I'm not sure I'm going to enjoy having sex with a pervert,' she told him, feeling marginally safer now behind the firmly locked bathroom door. 'I will never forgive you for not telling me about that dress, Will Saunders.'

'And I will never forgive you if you don't wear it again for me, Maggie Miller.' He was, she realised, enjoying this.

'Bring it with you today to my house. You can keep it there
and wear it just for me.'

'It's going to a charity shop.'

'I'll buy it.'

'Get your wonder-wife to wear it when you find her,'
she suggested crisply, pulling on her top. Checking her appearance in the mirror above the sink, she ran her fingers
through her hair to try to dry out the last of the moisture.
When it was as good as she could make it she twisted it
up on to the top of her head and clipped it.

Feeling more secure now, she opened the door to him.
'And I'm not going to your house,' she declared. 'I've
changed my mind.' Even if a little secret part of her delighted in his possessiveness as much as she found it ter-
rifying, it was important, she told herself firmly, that she
kept this under control. And the way to keep it under control was to assert herself now. She'd been like a jelly all
night, swaying and wobbling with his will and her desire.
It was time her brain took over.

'When you've organised whatever we need you might as
well come back here,' she told him. 'My bed's big enough
for two temporarily and at least that way I don't have to
drive home afterwards.'

To her surprise he looked quite taken aback at that.
'What are you talking about?'

'Sex,' she said evenly. 'Here. I thought. Rather than at
your house.'

'Sex?'

'Here.'

'What?'

'No reason why not.'

'You don't want to come into town?'

'Not especially.'

'What about tomorrow?'

'Well, if one of us does decide that he or she wants to

do it again a second time then you can come and see me tomorrow,' she said. 'Since you're on call you'll be driving out here in the morning anyway so it won't be a bother for you to detour here at some stage.'

'A bother?'

'I'll make lunch for you,' she told him. 'Oysters, perhaps, if the fish shop's open in the morning. They're supposed to be good before sex, aren't they?'

'Oysters?'

'Will, whatever is the matter?' Determined not to let him see how much behaving sensibly like this was costing her, Maggie tapped lightly at each of his cheeks with the back of her hand. 'You've gone quite pale.'

It was possible Maggie was teasing him. It was entirely possible, he told himself. In fact, he'd been sure of it at first, but when he'd laughed and tried to tease her out of it she'd seemed offended and now he didn't know again.

Maggie could be very serious at times and she was certainly playing it that way now. She'd obviously been annoyed he'd never warned her about that dress—that hadn't been faked—and that meant that this would be a perfect way of paying him back, he reflected. Only he wasn't quite sure that that was what she was doing.

If she was laughing at him then he deserved it, he acknowledged, his mouth softening into a wry smile. Even if he didn't like it. He'd been transparently manipulative, too mindless with desire for her to think of anything but getting her into his bed.

Not only that, his description of the phantom woman he was searching for to become his wife had been arrogant, inappropriate and ludicrously pompous. He slowed as he approached the hospital's entrance. He hadn't been called back but he'd needed to get away from her to get his thoughts straight and so had muttered some excuse and left.

Once or twice, he remembered, his mouth twitching. *If* either of them wanted a repeat experience. She had to know as well as he did that there was no way he was going to let her go once he had her. Perhaps not for... He frowned. Perhaps not for...months.

Then he remembered other things she'd said. Small things. Things that had seemed insignificant at the time. Earlier, when they'd argued outside the unit, she'd asked what would happen tomorrow or next week. She'd said something about it ending then, implying she meant their relationship.

And she'd been so determined that no one else should discover that they were lovers. At the time he'd thought he'd understood her concern—she'd been hurt by gossip at work after the break-up of her marriage—but the reason he hadn't considered secrecy an issue with them now was that he couldn't envisage a time when he wouldn't want her.

Clearly she envisaged a time when she'd no longer want him. And obviously that time was a lot closer than anything he'd anticipated. Not months away but tomorrow, he remembered. Or next week.

His head hurt. Mechanically he punched in the security code and headed upstairs. It was still early, before seven, but the nursing staff who'd be taking over the day shift had arrived and the unit was busy. Tim came over when Will was checking their new asthma admission.

'Nothing much exciting happening,' the younger man said. 'We need a new arterial line for Mr Jenkins. That one's due to go but we thought it could wait until the registrar on for today turns up. Unless you're desperate for something to do, that is. I thought you'd be enjoying a sleep-in.'

'I haven't even made it to bed yet,' he admitted absently, preoccupied.

Prue was obviously on duty for the morning because she

was back in uniform and she came up to them with a cheery grin. 'Merry Christmas, Will, you lovely man,' she said brightly, startling him with a quick but very bold kiss on his mouth. 'It's Christmas Day,' she said brightly, laughing at his quizzical look. 'We're allowed to take liberties. How did you like my truffles?'

'I'm saving them for a Christmas treat this morning,' he told her with a smile. 'The rumour is they're gorgeous.'

'Of course they are.' Prue had a paper or something similar for Tim to sign and she handed it to him. 'Speaking of gorgeous,' she teased, winking at Will before fluttering her eyelashes at the charge nurse. 'Sign my leave-request form, won't you, sweet pea?'

'With great reluctance,' Tim agreed, heaving a dramatic sigh and rolling his eyes as he scrawled his signature. 'How long this time?'

'Only two weeks. John's taking me to Fiji.' When he handed the form back to her she thanked him with an extravagantly blown kiss. 'Thank you, my angel, you are a darling. I'm happy to get caught with you in the equipment room any time.'

Will laughed and Prue grinned at him as she danced off, but Tim's expression was wry. 'It's not a joke,' he complained. 'It happens all the time.'

'Prue's a very happily married woman,' Will observed.

'Prue is, but not all of them are. Women these days,' Tim said, shaking his head. 'All they want is sex.'

Even if Tim was only joking, his words echoed Will's own concerns about Maggie too closely for him to be comfortable with them, and he frowned briefly and looked away.

'You think I'm joking,' Tim said lightly. 'Well, I'm not.' The younger man flexed a carefully muscled arm. 'Look at this body. They can't leave me alone. I'm afraid to go into the equipment room. It happens here and it happens every time I go out anywhere. They can't get enough of me.'

Will regarded him blandly. 'Tim—'

'I really am not joking,' the nurse declared. 'I'm exhausted. Why do you think I keep wanting to work nights?'

'The money?' Will ventured.

'To get a rest.' Tim shook his head ruefully. 'I keep telling myself that one day I'm going to meet a nice girl who wants to settle down and raise children with me, but it's just not happening. All the ones I meet love their jobs. All they're interested in is sex.'

Will thought about Maggie. 'Women aren't so ruthless. There must be a least some emotional involvement for them, mustn't there?'

'Maggie giving you trouble, is she?'

Will said heavily, 'I'm going to forget you said that.'

'Understood.' But the nurse winked. 'Women have changed, Will. Get with it. They know what they want. We men have got to get used to it.'

One of the other nurses called Tim away then, leaving Will alone with his thoughts.

He recognised that he had no right to make demands of Maggie but that didn't mean he didn't want to. His hands curled into fists on the chart he was pretending to study. The thought that he might have reawakened her interest in sex enough for her to then go carelessly and unemotionally from him to another man made him sick. So where did that leave him?

CHAPTER ELEVEN

MAGGIE gave Will a good start on her so he could get whatever it was he wanted to do on the ward out of the way before their round. It was still early but the sky was blue and the air was warm and it was obviously going to be a beautifully clear and hot day.

As she stepped out onto the path between the flats and the hospital proper the sun slid between the narrow fronds of a cabbage tree and touched her eyes. She tilted her face up to it, loving its warmth and brightness.

She took a few long, deep breaths then laughed out loud, her face alive. Her arms outstretched to the day, she spun around. For the first time in as long as she could remember she felt suddenly, violently and passionately glad to be alive.

Will was in the unit with Mr Jenkins, one of their surgical patients, a man with severe pancreatitis, or inflammation of the pancreas. He'd been stable for the last few days, slowly recovering, she'd thought. She was so worried that Will might be with him because something had gone wrong overnight she went across.

He was simply inserting a fresh arterial line. Gloved and masked, his head was lowered and he was obviously concentrating. Smoothly, and without faltering, he slid the small cannula into place.

There was a fresh heparinised bag of saline ready and the fluid had been purged through its line. As soon as he had the cannula positioned where he wanted it she passed the end of the line towards him, holding the non-sterile part of it so that he could connect the sterile bit. 'I like watching you do these,' she said quietly. 'I've never seen anyone make them seem so effortless.'

'Practice.' He looked up briefly, his regard, she realised, tensing, cooler than usual, neutral—*assessing* almost. 'Tim was here helping me but he raced off somewhere. Would you pass me that dressing, please?'

'Of course.' Obediently she tore open the sterile pack, holding it so that he could lift out the dressing itself. 'Is something wrong?'

'Nothing obviously.' He covered the cannula and the start of the line with the transparent dressing, then twisted a length of line into a loop and taped it so that it couldn't be pulled out accidentally. 'Mrs Adams has had a good night. Mr Radcliffe's awake enough this morning to signal ''Merry Christmas'' to us so Tim's called the family to suggest they all come in. Mrs Everett's awake—no problems getting her tube out—Mr Fale looks much better and our new asthma admission's improving.'

He pulled his gloves off then leaned across to the pump close to where she stood and pressed a button which made it whirr into action. 'Reihana Te Huia's the registrar on call today and Peter Finch is the consultant but neither of them is in yet. We should wait until they're here to go around.'

'Of course we should.' She didn't understand why he was even bothering to say that to her because at weekends and holidays it was strict unit protocol for the medical staff going off to hand over to the doctors coming on. They never started the formal round until the others arrived.

'Will...?' She wasn't sure what she wanted to say but already some of her morning's euphoria was beginning to leach out of her bones.

He wasn't paying her any attention. He'd tugged his mask down and his expression was calm, but he was preoccupied with clearing up the trolley he'd been using. 'Back in a minute,' he said, taking it away.

She followed him to the utility room. 'Have I done something wrong?' she asked nervously, once the door had swung shut behind them. Half an hour ago he'd been laughing and kissing her. Now, somehow, he'd withdrawn.

'No. Not at all.' But a faint stiffness in his expression told her that he was not as unaware of her bewilderment as she'd thought. Leaving the trolley, he came to her, held her shoulders and kissed her very gently on her forehead. 'You're wonderful. Gorgeous. As always.'

'But there's something,' she protested.

'A few questions.' He tilted his head. 'What do you really see happening afterwards, Maggie?'

'That doesn't sound like your sort of question.' She'd spoken lightly but his expression didn't change and she realised that he was serious now. Her throat felt suddenly very dry and she swallowed heavily. 'You're supposed to leave worrying about afterwards to me,' she pointed out huskily, clasping her hands behind her. 'In fact, I thought we'd already established that I specialise in that particular neurosis.'

'Humour me,' he said deeply.

'I'm sure we'll be able to work together,' she said carefully. 'For me, as I've told you, that will be a lot easier if no one else knows.' She caught her lower lip between her teeth, thinking. 'There might be awkward moments from time to time but that should be all.'

'And other men?'

'What?'

'You and other men,' he said flatly.

'I'm not interested in other men,' she said slowly, not understanding what he was asking. 'There's not one I can even think of—'

'How about Tim?' Ignoring her recoil, he persisted. 'Won't you want to have sex with Tim?'

'No!' She shook her head vaguely. 'Of course not.'

'Don't you find him attractive?'

'He's very attractive,' she admitted. 'And a lovely person. I'm very fond of Tim but I don't want to sleep with him.'

'Why not?'

Maggie frowned, still bewildered. 'Will, I know I've been behaving like some sort of sex maniac—'

His regard sharpened. 'Is that how you see yourself?'

'Well…in the lift.' She felt herself flushing. 'I got a little…carried away. If the doors hadn't been about to open I don't think I'd have wanted to stop.'

'And when you felt like that, did it matter who I was?'

'If I'd been with any other man I'd never have felt like that in the first place,' she whispered, wondering faintly how he could possibly doubt that.

He didn't move and his expression didn't change but she felt something in him relax, and she realised, startled because she'd been sure his confidence must be supreme, that he'd doubted her feelings.

'Maggie, how many times do you think I want to make love to you?'

'I don't know.' She lifted one shoulder uncertainly. 'How many times were *you* thinking?'

'Were you serious when you said *if* we wanted to repeat things tomorrow?'

'Partly,' she admitted. 'But I thought that I probably…well, I thought tomorrow I probably still would be interested. In fact, I think I definitely will be interested. That is, if you are, too.'

'Of course I'll bloody be interested.' He came forward and kissed her. 'Didn't Graham want sex often?'

'We were working very long hours,' she said huskily. 'Sometimes we'd hardly see each other for weeks.'

'Ball park.'

'Ball park…about…' She hesitated, but it was hard to

remember. 'Ball park, probably...probably most months. At the beginning at least. Not so often later.'

'Most months?' He looked aghast. 'Most *months*?'

'Is that bad?'

'It explains one or two things that have been puzzling me,' he said rawly. 'You really do have no idea.'

'I have lots of ideas.'

'Maggie, I want to take you to bed a hundred times.' He pulled her against him again, his hand holding the back of her head so her face was pressed to the warm, fragrant skin of his throat above his shirt. 'A thousand times. Ten thousand times. A hundred thousand times.'

'That's not going to give you much time to find wonder-wife,' she breathed, pressing her mouth to the warm hollow between his collarbones.

'She'll turn up,' he said carelessly, hugging her. 'Some time.'

'More kisses.' She arched herself against him, delighting in the soft sound he made in his throat as her breasts grazed his chest. 'Please.'

'Not yet.' His voice was ragged but he put her away. 'I have to clear this up.' His eyes promised her the world but he'd moved back to the trolley. 'Then there's breakfast. Then the round. Then there's time.'

'The nurses will be wondering what we're doing here,' she said huskily, flushing as his words reminded her of where they were. She backed towards the door. 'I'll go check that that line is still all right.'

His cry as she pulled the door shut brought her flying back in again. 'What is it?' she demanded. 'What's wrong?'

'Needle stick,' he replied grimly. As she watched he pulled out the small needle he'd managed to stick into his finger. They both stared at the slowly bleeding wound. 'My mind must have been... I can't believe I could be so bloody stupid,' he raged, dabbing at the blood with a paper towel from the dispenser attached to the wall. 'There's a sharps-disposal box right there on the trolley. How the hell could I have left one just sitting there?'

'Let it bleed,' Maggie said urgently. She snatched the towel away and threw it towards the rubbish. Her hands were shaking. In anything like this there was a risk of transferring disease.

Mr Jenkins was a chronic alcoholic who had a repeated history of bleeding from the fragile blood vessels around the top of his stomach. He'd had dozens of transfusions over the years, and though they'd tested him for HIV and the three main types of hepatitis infection there were other infections they couldn't test for.

Working automatically because she could barely think, she turned on the warm water in the sink and held his finger under the stream to encourage it to bleed. 'We need iodine to clean it.'

'There's some on the shelf.' With his other hand he reached above her head and brought down a brown bottle of solution. 'I can't believe I could be such an idiot. It's years since I've done this to myself.'

'I never have,' she said thickly. 'I'm too paranoid.'

'We all should be.' He'd stopped bleeding now and he held his finger out for her to run iodine over it. 'Has he been tested?'

'HIV and Hep A through C,' she confirmed. 'But if you were going to stick yourself from anybody he was definitely not the best candidate to choose. We'll have to report you to Occupational Health. Was it the actual needle you used for the arterial puncture?'

'The local.'

While she was busy still washing him she could feel him doing something with the trolley with his other hand. Then he pulled free, his face abruptly relieved.

'Relax,' he said flatly. 'It's all right.' He kissed her

mouth hard. 'It's the needle I used to draw up the local. I used a smaller one to inject it and I disposed of that one properly. It's safe. There's no risk.'

'Oh, thank God.' Maggie felt her whole body soften. 'Oh, help.' She sagged back against the sink, breathing fast. 'Goodness. I think I'm going to faint.'

'Sit down.' He swung a chair around and guided her into it. 'Put your head down. You're so pale. You're worse than me.'

'I couldn't think straight,' she breathed. 'I was panicking.'

'It was just a needle stick.'

'I know but…well, I was worried,' she said weakly, breathing deeply. Her head swam and she leaned right forward, letting it drop between her knees. 'Oh, dear. I don't want to go through that again. Please, please, don't ever do that to me again. Please be careful next time. Please be careful every single time.'

'It's not just sex,' he said quietly. 'That's why you're so sure you don't want anybody else. You're in love with me.'

His words slammed into her like a heavy weight and she felt as if every ounce of blood in her body drained immediately into her chest. She couldn't breathe. She felt sick. 'No.'

'Yes, you are.' She had her head lowered so she couldn't see him, but she could hear his confidence and it terrified her. 'You love me,' he said calmly. 'You must. To react like this you must.'

Slowly, very slowly, she lifted her head, keeping her face fiercely controlled. 'Just because I don't want you to get sick—'

'It's more than that. I don't know why it's taken me so long to realise. It's the only thing that makes sense.'

'Will…?' She moistened her lips, barely able to breathe. 'No.'

'You fought me so hard and for so long.' His hand brushed softly across her cheek and to her despair she found her mouth turning involuntarily, betrayingly, into his caress. 'But you changed your mind after just one kiss.'

'It was a pretty amazing one,' she said weakly.

'But, then, we both always knew it would be.' He cupped her face properly. 'It was always going to be good between us. That's what the magic is.' He kissed her fiercely then lifted his head. 'Don't pretend, Maggie. Not now.'

'Will...?' Of course he was right. She loved him. It wasn't easy and she'd never wanted it or planned it but there was nothing she could do about it. She simply had to live with it and hope that one day it would go away. 'Does...does it matter?'

'I don't know. I have to think. It should matter, shouldn't it? It should change things. But I don't know.'

Her head felt muzzy and noisy but she couldn't stay here now. It was too awful. She didn't want him to see her like this. Ignoring the half-hearted way he raised one arm to delay her, she escaped out into the unit proper.

Tim was there, and he slung his arm across the back of her shoulders. 'Come to breakfast,' he ordered. 'It's all ready. What's Will up to?'

'He's sorting things,' she said vaguely, turning her head. 'What breakfast?'

'Christmas breakfast in the staffroom. It's a special occasion. We've got champagne. And you can't get out of it,' he ordered, obviously interpreting her expression, 'because we will be mortally offended. This way.'

The nurses had gone to a lot of trouble. There was champagne, as Tim had promised, and he ignored her protests and forced a plastic tumbler of it into one of her trembling hands.

They had strawberries and passion-fruit and kiwis and punnets of fat, juicy boysenberries. There was a platter of smoked salmon and trout, with some oysters, and another of New Zealand cheeses, together with breads, mince pies and chocolates. Tim put some of everything onto a paper plate, gave it to Maggie with a fork and put her into a seat in the corner by the window. 'Eat,' he ordered.

'I should have brought something,' she said vaguely. 'I didn't realise.'

'We took half the money out of petty cash,' Prue told her brightly. 'As we weren't allowed to spend it on Christmas decorations, we thought we'd spend it on Christmas food.'

'Will paid for the rest,' Tim told her cheerfully. 'I was telling him about how we didn't even have time for a drink last year. He must have felt sorry for us because he wasn't even rostered to be here today.' He lifted his tumbler. 'A toast in his absence. Cheers, Will.'

'Cheers.' There was a chorus of happy echoes into which Maggie joined as neutrally as she could manage.

She was still shaking. She took an absent mouthful of her drink, then ate a couple of boysenberries, barely managing to exchange a few words with Prue about something the other woman had seen on television a few nights before. Nothing felt real.

Even if she hadn't felt Will's presence, the nurses' greetings would have told her he was there. She refused to look at him, although she could feel his eyes on her face like a physical touch, and concentrated on her food, carefully rolling up one thin slice of smoked salmon with her fork.

He said a few things, general Christmas greetings and a wish that they enjoyed the meal. The conversation sounded normal, but she could feel him looking at her all the while.

'Maggie…?' He was at the other end of the table—near the door where she was against the window at the far end—but his soft, insistent command was as compelling as if he'd been directly beside her. 'Come here. I want to talk to you.'

'I'm eating.' She looked at him then, keeping her face guarded.

It felt as if they were alone in the universe, even though there was enough conversation and laughter going on for them to speak privately.

'We can do this your way or we can do it my way,' he told her quietly. 'If you don't come with me now then it's my way.'

'Your way, then.' She didn't know what he was talking about but she knew she wasn't going to move from the relative protection the nurses provided around her. She'd already humiliated herself in front of him by her reaction in the clinical room and what had happened afterwards. She needed time to get herself together, before being alone with him again. 'We can talk later.'

'Later isn't good enough.' He stood, the movement drawing the attention of everyone else, and most of them raised their glasses, obviously expecting another toast.

But to her horror he was still looking at her. 'Last chance, Maggie.'

She looked back at her food, blinking quickly, willing him not to say anything but too shaken to move.

'Maggie Miller, I love you,' he announced. The room immediately dissolved into a tight, incredulous, appalling silence. 'I adore you. I want you for ever.'

She shut her eyes sickly. 'Will, don't.'

'When I think about sticking myself with that needle all I think is that I don't want to get sick because that would mean I might miss out on my life because my life is you.'

'No.'

'I'll never want any woman other than you. I want to live with you for ever. I want you to be the mother of my children. I want you to marry me.'

'You are certifiably insane,' she whispered, unbearably

conscious that they held the spellbound attention of every single person in the room.

'It's Christmas Day. If you turn me down now all these lovely people are going to feel sorry for me always,' he continued. 'Every Christmas here they'll remember and they'll feel sorry for me and I'll be old and sad and lonely and no one will ever forget how you rejected me.'

'Don't.'

'I love you.'

'What about wonder-wife?' she groaned.

'I don't want her. She'd bore me silly. I want you.'

'Stop it.'

'For God's sake, Maggie.' Tim's grin, like every other in the room, was about a foot wide. 'Put the poor man out of his misery.'

'Imagine them, feeling sorry for me,' Will intoned gruffly.

'You're a manipulative, blackmailing, horrible man,' she whispered. 'I will hate you for ever for this.'

'But you love me.'

She hung her head. 'Yes.'

He came for her amidst the tables and the chairs and the food and the nurses and their laughter and their cheers and congratulations, and he lifted her into his arms and carried her out. 'I also came to say that Reihana and Peter have arrived,' he said softly. 'Steven?' he called, outraging Maggie who'd assumed he felt as dazed as her while instead he'd probably had his mind on his work all the time. 'Drop the food. Ward round.'

Laughing at her protests, he took her all the way into the unit, releasing her only when an astonished-looking Reihana and the consultant taking over their shift had seen them.

'Maggie's going to marry me,' he declared confidently,

although she'd definitely never agreed to that. 'We're starting our celebrations early.'

'Before or after you ruin my life for ever?' Maggie complained, dusting herself down, miserably resigned to becoming the major topic of conversation for the entire ICU staff for at least the next six weeks. 'I'm not going to marry you, Will Saunders, so don't take anything for granted. At this moment we are barely even friends.'

Ignoring his dancing eyes and struggling for a business-like demeanour, she strode towards Mr Radcliffe's bed, supremely conscious of them all trailing behind her. 'Just because it's Christmas Day doesn't mean there's not work to be done.'

'Because I've already been married and I didn't like it,' she snapped, for what seemed the umpteenth time, two hours later as he drove off the motorway that had led them down the coast then curved down and around along the sun-drenched harbour into Wellington. 'Loving you doesn't change that. If it's that important to you then we'll live together.'

They'd slowed for traffic and he sent her another one of his very blue, very exasperated looks. 'You've had a bad experience but now it's time to forget that because you're about to have a good one. You'll like our marriage.'

'There won't be an *ours*.' She folded her arms and stared out of the window. 'I still don't know why I'm even here with you now. We could have had sex at my place.'

'We're not going to have sex, Maggie.' He spoke with the same type of heavily emphasised patience he'd been using for the past two hours and she was beginning to find it supremely irritating. 'We're going to make love. There's a wonderful difference. Just like there's a wonderful difference between living together and marriage.'

'I never realised you were so conventional.'

'I'm not.' He sent her a briefly assessing look. 'The truth is, I'm surprising myself on this.'

'You're too used to getting your own way.'

'You're too used to getting yours.'

'I'm not going to marry you.'

His house was lovely. Old and wooden, it stood high on a leafy hill close to the university, overlooking the city and its magnificent harbour. The floors were polished wood so she took her shoes off at the door then padded in her bare feet across to the living room's wide windows, catching her breath at the view. 'It's beautiful.'

'I'm glad you like it.' She heard the sounds of his keys being dropped onto a table and then he was behind her, his hands sliding around to cup her breasts. 'Let's get rid of this,' he murmured, tugging at her top. 'Hmm?'

'Yes, please.' She lifted her arms so that he could tug it over her head, then shut her eyes when his mouth closed over her. She wound her hands into his hair, holding him to her, entranced by the delicate, erotic tugging of his mouth at her breast.

When he shifted her eyes blinked open in protest but his warm regard was knowing and gentle and she realised that he wasn't leaving her, simply taking her to the comfortable-looking couch in the corner.

Silently, he tugged her down to him so that she sat across him with her thighs straddling his hips, and to her delight he cupped her breasts again, his darkly flushed face lowering as he sucked one tiny nipple back into his mouth.

Abrupt need flooded her. She bit hard down on her lower lip, trying to control herself—but she couldn't. The area between her thighs felt swollen and tender and she gripped his shoulders and lifted herself against him, unconsciously moving in time with the rhythmic movements of his tongue against her breast. Her heart beat so heavily that she could feel it throbbing inside her chest. 'Will...?'

'Mmm?'

'Please...?'

He smiled. Seeming to understand what she wanted, his hands shifted from her breasts and slid beneath the waist-band of her trousers and under the elastic of her panties to cup her buttocks. He pulled her forward, rocking her, the pressure of his arousal so hard between her splayed thighs that even through their clothes the pressure on her was ex-quisite. 'Like this?' he asked softly, his mouth at her breast again.

'Yes.' Maggie felt dizzy. She was hot and dazed and her hands and legs were shaking and she knew that what she was doing should be embarrassing her but somehow it wasn't and she couldn't stop herself.

'Marry me?'

She shook her head mutely, concentrating on the sharp-ening sensations from her breasts and from the pressure between her legs, his words an irritating intrusion.

But he stopped. So swiftly she barely understood what was happening, he shifted, scooping her up and depositing her on her feet away from him.

'I'm going to take a shower and change into some fresh clothes,' he remarked, his breathing still fast but his tone so completely even that she blinked up at him, dazed. 'Feel free to have a look around if you're curious.' Leaving her speechless and bereft and feeling utterly abandoned, he walked out.

It took her a while to collect herself but when she had she followed the sound of running water upstairs. Despite the glass walls of the shower cubicle being misted and opaque, she didn't feel quite brave enough to venture into the bathroom and she hesitated in the open doorway. 'Will, that's cheap blackmail,' she cried, speaking loudly so he'd hear her over the noise of the water. 'I'm not going to give in to that.'

'What?' he yelled.

She went closer. 'I said I'm not going to give in to that.'

'What?'

'I said—' But as she stepped fractionally nearer, her mouth drying at the thought of him being naked and so close, a soapy arm came out from the shower and he dragged her under the water.

'I wouldn't have said *cheap* blackmail,' he murmured, laughing at her squeals and easily containing her struggles with his arms and his body. 'You can't even begin to imagine how much this is costing me.'

Maggie knew how much it was costing her. He was glorious. Muscled and strong and aroused, he made her head swim, and her struggles eased as she realised that she didn't want to escape. 'You're seducing me,' she whispered.

'Of course I am,' he murmured. 'I've been seducing you for eleven months.' He bit gently at her ear. 'Only now my intentions are honourable.'

Maggie ignored that. 'Will, I have to get out of here.' His body was shielding her from the bulk of the water but she was still getting wet. She gestured vaguely at the rapidly dampening top, which she'd put on again downstairs, and her pants. 'I haven't any spare clothes.'

'That's all right. I don't want you to wear any. You're not going anywhere.' He removed her top, by hauling it over her head, then flung it out of the cubicle. 'Now these awful things,' he said firmly, lifting her briefly so that he could tug away her trousers, which promptly followed the path of her top, landing on the tiled floor outside with a heavy, sodden slap.

'I like these,' he murmured, cupping her teasingly through the damp, red satin of her panties. 'Sexy. They can stay. But not this.' He tugged at her hair clip and threw it out to follow her clothes, then he twisted her, holding her so that she stood directly beneath the warm water blinking away the trickles that streamed across her face, while he brought down her hair and soaked it until it lay drenched and heavy around her shoulders.

Imprisoned by the weight of his body, she tried to speak but he hushed her with his mouth, lingering, tender, achingly wonderful kisses flavoured with the water that cascaded on and between them. He caressed her breasts and her head, but he didn't let her touch him, catching the seeking hands she lifted to his chest and holding them behind her so she couldn't reach him.

Still holding her, he took coconut-scented soap from the rack above her head and soaped her, starting at first innocently with long exquisite strokes upwards from her thighs, across her hips and up to her arms. But then he slid his soapy hand under the elastic of her panties in an intimate, probing, wonderful caress that left her melting again.

'Going to marry me?'

'No.'

She had her eyes closed but he must have adjusted the tap because his hand withdrew and the water turned abruptly ice-cold. Her eyes blinked open sharply but she saw his amusement and gritted her teeth, refusing to give him the satisfaction of containing her struggles again. Very, very, briefly, she let her gaze flicker to the physical and disturbing evidence of his arousal. 'Funny. Funny. Sooner or later,' she grated stiffly, 'you're going to get very uncomfortable if you don't give in to this.'

But he just laughed. 'Maggie, you've been doing this to me for eleven months,' he said softly, kissing her chin. 'I can manage a little longer.' He turned off the water and carried her into a bedroom and dumped her, still wet and dripping, onto the bed. Then he came after her, his mouth warm on her stomach, his hands, to her horror, firmly separating her damp thighs.

Automatically her hand lowered to shield herself. 'I'm

not going to marry you,' she said hoarsely. 'It doesn't matter what you do. Being in love doesn't have to mean getting married.'

'But I want it to.' He took her hand away then held her firmly when she tried to roll away, one arm going across to hold her flat while his other hand gently caressed and stroked her until she was weak and soft and wet and longing for him again.

'Don't stop,' she whispered desperately.

But his fingers slowed. 'Marry me.'

She caught her breath, mentally begging him to continue. 'I'll think about it.'

His laugh was warm and husky against her stomach. 'I'm not your sex object, Maggie, my love.' To her dismay the caress stopped, but he wasn't leaving her again, merely turning to kneel above her. He smoothed protection on himself then fitted himself between her splayed legs, his hands sliding beneath her buttocks to hold her steady where she might otherwise have moved against him. 'I won't let you play games with me. Marry me. Tell me now.'

The sweet, teasing pressure of him against her was the most exquisite thing she'd ever felt and she ached for more. 'Cheap...blackmail,' she breathed.

'Good, isn't it?' His face was flushed and taut but he was still laughing at her as he eased himself slowly and insistently into her. The reality of his possession turned her insides to liquid and at that moment of joy she realised that she was completely and utterly his. But suddenly, instead of the passion and movement her body craved, he was still. 'Tell me now,' he ordered thickly. 'Tell me, Maggie, or there's nothing else.'

She believed him. He was inside her, gripped tightly with her muscles, breathing hard, obviously aroused, but his expression was steely and his determination warned her that he remained in complete control of both of them.

'Say yes.' His fingers parted her above where they were joined revealing her most sensitive point, and he looked away from her face and down at her, his chest rising with effort as he stayed intent on her, watching her as he moved, thrusting softly, slowly, the chafing movement so delicate that it had to be calculated to drive her mad with frustration.

'Yes. All right, yes.' She practically shouted the words. 'Yes.'

'About bloody time,' he muttered, his kiss hard and fiercely possessive as he thrust into her, cannoning them both sweetly into ecstasy.

Later, curled sweat-damp and naked in his arms, Maggie pressed a kiss to his shoulder. 'You know I could have held out longer,' she lied drowsily, teasing him. 'I'm not completely in your power.'

His hand curled languidly around her breast. 'I probably could have held off another ten seconds or so myself.'

'Ten seconds?' She sat up. 'What?'

'I suspect you overestimate my control,' he said, tugging her down to him again, laughing. 'Be rational, Maggie. I've waited a long time for you. Forget what I told you—there was no way I was going to be able to stop myself.'

'You tricked me!'

'I had no choice.' He kissed her nose and then her eyes and her cheeks and her chin. 'You drove me to it with your stubbornness.'

'I'm not going to have a big wedding.'

'I love your ears,' he murmured, kissing one. 'Five or six hundred.'

'Five or six hundred?' Horrified, she sat up again. 'You're joking. I've only got my mother and Patrick.'

'My family, friends, colleagues, all of the ICU staff,' he reeled off, coming to face her, punctuating each word with a light, frustrating brush of his tongue across her breast.

'There're some friends in England who'll want to come out.'

Maggie struggled up onto her knees, pushing him away. 'Will, no,' she said fiercely. 'Absolutely no. No way on earth. Never. I couldn't bear it.'

'Well, what's your idea?' Intent on her breasts, he was back at them already. 'Four hundred? Three hundred? What do you think? Hmm?'

'A couple of witnesses. A dozen family.' She shook her head, thinking. 'Some flowers. A garden or a beach. Something like that. Something very quiet and very plain.'

He went very still. 'So you haven't changed your mind? You're definitely saying yes?'

'Yes.' It came out in a little whisper.

'I adore you.' He captured her mouth in a long, achingly possessive kiss.

She stroked his cheek. 'My life without you was incomplete.'

'Except for your fantasies.'

After a few seconds of stunned silence Maggie flushed violently. 'I should never have mentioned that,' she said faintly. 'I can't believe I ever said anything.'

'Too late now,' he teased, laughing. 'You know I had to have you after you told me that. I think if I hadn't I'd never have had an undisturbed night's sleep again.'

'They weren't anything weird,' she said slowly, still flushing. 'Just daydreams. Just, well…you know, you wearing a fireman's uniform and things like that.'

'A fireman's uniform.' He grinned at her. 'I've a brother who's a fireman. I can get a fireman's uniform.'

But she didn't want that. 'Making love with you was better than anything I've ever fantasised about,' she said softly. 'Can we leave the fireman bit until our seven-year itch?'

'Then what about our fourteen-year itch?'

'Well, there was this other one about you being my gardener,' she confessed. 'We could try that one then if we need something.' She touched his smiling mouth. 'There is no one and nothing more precious to me in this world than you.'

'Ah, no. Before you can say that you have to try one of *my* fantasies.' He swung off the bed and left the room. She heard him go downstairs and she waited, puzzled. He came back a few moments later with something dark and squishy in his hand. He put it to her mouth. 'Bite.'

Maggie bit. It was creamy and chocolatey and utterly wonderful. 'I can't believe it,' she said huskily. 'That's the most fantastic thing I've ever tasted.'

'Prue's truffles,' he said smugly. 'I saved you one. I told you you'd love it.'

'Better than sex,' she breathed.

'Witch!' Urgent now, he tumbled her back into the covers, his mouth licking greedily at the tiny flakes of chocolate still clinging around her lips. 'Maggie Miller, prepare yourself to be forced to eat those words.'

Maggie laughed, giving herself up blissfully to passion. 'I'll have the truffles at Christmas and you every other day,' she teased.

'You'll have me every day for ever,' he promised. 'And more times than you can possibly count every single Christmas Day anniversary for the rest of your life.'

MILLS & BOON®

*M*akes
any time
special

Copyright © Harlequin Enterprises Limited 1997
All rights reserved

Enjoy a romantic novel from
Mills & Boon®

Presents™ *Enchanted*™ *Temptation*®

Historical Romance™ *Medical Romance*™

MILLS & BOON®

Medical Romance™

COMING NEXT MONTH

SARAH'S GIFT by Caroline Anderson
Audley Memorial Hospital

Having lost her own family, Sarah loved having Matt Ryan
and his little girl, Emily, living with her while they were in
England. She didn't know that Matt had an inestimable
gift for her...

POTENTIAL DADDY by Lucy Clark

Kathryn wasn't sure she liked the professional Jack—brilliant
and arrogant—but his private side was a revelation. He'd
make the perfect father, but who would he choose as the
mother of his potential children?

LET TOMORROW COME by Rebecca Lang

Gerard came to Jan's help when she most needed it, but she
found it so hard to trust, she was sure he'd have a hidden
agenda. How could he convince her that he hadn't?

THE PATIENT MAN by Margaret O'Neill

Harry Paradine knew if he was patient enough that the right
woman would come along. When she finally did, he found
Emily Prince less than trustful—but why?

*Available at most branches of WH Smith, Tesco, Asda,
Martins, Borders, Easons, Volume One/James Thin
and most good paperback bookshops*

MILLS & BOON®

Next Month's Romance Titles

♡

Each month you can choose from a wide variety of romance novels from Mills & Boon®. Below are the new titles to look out for next month from the Presents™ and Enchanted™ series.

Presents™

TO WOO A WIFE	Carole Mortimer
CONTRACT BABY	Lynne Graham
IN BED WITH THE BOSS	Susan Napier
SURRENDER TO SEDUCTION	Robyn Donald
OUTBACK MISTRESS	Lindsay Armstrong
THE SECRET DAUGHTER	Catherine Spencer
THE MARRIAGE ASSIGNMENT	Alison Kelly
WIFE BY AGREEMENT	Kim Lawrence

Enchanted™

BE MY GIRL!	Lucy Gordon
LONESOME COWBOY	Debbie Macomber
A SUITABLE GROOM	Liz Fielding
NEW YEAR...NEW FAMILY	Grace Green
OUTBACK HUSBAND	Jessica Hart
MAKE-BELIEVE MOTHER	Pamela Bauer & Judy Kaye
OH, BABY!	Lauryn Chandler
FOLLOW THAT GROOM!	Christie Ridgway

On sale from 8th January 1999

H1 9812

Available at most branches of WH Smith, Tesco, Asda, Martins, Borders and all good paperback bookshops

MILLS & BOON

Relive the romance with

Bestselling themed romances brought back to you by popular demand

Each month By Request brings you three full-length novels in one beautiful volume featuring the best of the best.

So if you missed a favourite Romance the first time around, here is your chance to relive the magic from some of our most popular authors.

Look out for
Christmas Masquerades in December 1998
**featuring Emma Darcy,
Debbie Macomber and Ann Charlton**

*Available at most branches of WH Smith,
Tesco, Asda, Martins, Borders and
all good paperback bookshops*

We are giving away a year's supply of Mills & Boon® books to the five lucky winners of our latest competition. Simply match the six film stars to the films in which they appeared, complete the coupon overleaf and send this entire page to us by 30th June 1999. The first five correct entries will each win a year's subscription to the Mills & Boon series of their choice. What could be easier?

CABARET	__	**GONE WITH THE WIND**	__
ROCKY	__	**SMOKEY & THE BANDIT**	__
PRETTY WOMAN	__	**GHOST**	__

C8L

Please turn over for details of how to enter ➡

HOW TO ENTER

There are six famous faces and a list of six films overleaf. Each of the famous faces starred in one of the films listed and all you have to do is match them up!

As you match each one, write the number of the actor or actress who starred in each film in the space provided. When you have matched them all, fill in the coupon below, pop this page in an envelope and post it today. Don't forget you could win a year's supply of Mills & Boon® books—you don't even need to pay for a stamp!

Mills & Boon Hollywood Heroes Competition
FREEPOST CN81, Croydon, Surrey, CR9 3WZ
EIRE readers: (please affix stamp) PO Box 4546, Dublin 24.

Please tick the series you would like to receive if you
are one of the lucky winners

Presents™ ❑ Enchanted™ ❑ Historical Romance™ ❑
Medical Romance™ ❑ Temptation® ❑

Are you a Reader Service™ subscriber?   Yes ❑   No ❑

Ms/Mrs/Miss/Mr ....Initials ....
(BLOCK CAPITALS PLEASE)

Surname...

Address ....

....

....Postcode..........................

(I am over 18 years of age)   C8L

Closing date for entries is 30th June 1999. One entry per household. Free subscriptions are for four books per month. Competition open to residents of the UK and Ireland only. As a result of this application, you may receive further offers from Harlequin Mills & Boon and other carefully selected companies. If you would prefer not to share in this opportunity please write to The Data Manager at the address shown above.

Mills & Boon is a registered trademark of
Harlequin Mills & Boon Ltd.